A QUIET DEATH...

Now the convocation audience would begin to file out, the front rows first. Dr. Grace Forrester suspected she should wait till the crush was over....

Really, why couldn't people file out in an orderly fashion? There was a lady in the second, left-front row, aisle seat, obstructing traffic. She seemed unwilling to leave, and equally unwilling to rise and let others go by. It was really extraordinary behavior! And some others were now gathering around her, rather than just squeezing past. From five rows back Grace watched the small group forming concentric rings, as a pearl is formed around the grain of sand that serves as the original irritant.

The simile had indeed been apt. Slumped over in one of the green plush seats reserved for minor dignitaries was a woman, as annoying in death as she had been irritating in life....

...A CONVENIENT DEATH

A CONVENIENT DEATH

Ruth Galbraith

PaperJacks LTD.

TORONTO   NEW YORK

AN ORIGINAL

PaperJacks

A CONVENIENT DEATH

PaperJacks LTD.

330 Steelcase Rd. E., Markham, Ont. L3R 2M1
210 Fifth Ave., New York, N.Y. 10010

PaperJacks publication December 1986

ISBN 0-7701-0500-9

For Peter

A CONVENIENT DEATH

CHAPTER ONE

She settled stiffly into her seat, looking around at the
people slowly filling up the vast gymnasium. At least
retirement meant one could select which convocations one
would attend, she mused, thinking back over all those she
had had to participate in over the years in her official
capacity. She supposed that there had been a more emi-
nent speaker on a previous occasion, but this was the first
time one of her ex-students was to address convocation,
and that made this year's event very special to her.

Jamie had always had the ability to hold an audience,
she remembered, even in the early days when he was
taking his turn leading an undergraduate seminar. She
called back a mental picture of him: a little ungainly, his
hair ruffled as he gestured, the suit sleeve sliding back from
the bony, boyish wrist. One might not have suspected then
that a farm boy would be able to command such attention
from his fellow students, but he could spellbind them. He
had always sounded so very plausible, his arguments, on
the surface, so very convincing. Of course, he had been
basically a very sound student, goal-oriented, willing to
work hard, and his subsequent career had certainly served
to disprove those vague suspicions at the time that he had
"short-circuited" one of his courses . . . oh, how long ago
that was, anyway. That must have been in the mid-forties,
she thought, that rumor about his biology course, and look

where he was now! Why did memory maintain an iron grip on trivia while clutching desperately for important facts just out of reach, flotsam drifting beyond its scrabbling fingers?

It remained a source of wonder to her that while some brilliant students melded contentedly and quietly into the academic milieu, others, not necessarily more able, felt a compelling need to sound their trumpets on a broader plain. She was sure that Jamie's very secure perch on the top research rung of a multinational drug company had not been attained without the inevitable strewing of bodies from the lower rungs of the competitive ladder. Perhaps his compulsion to succeed at any cost stemmed from that austere background, from that righteous, rigorous father. Would he now be proud of Jamie or, as it said on the program: "J. Richardson Dewar, B.A. (Lockland), M.A. (Yale), PH D (Columbia)"?

Her thoughts veered. Times change, and one had to progress with them, but surely convocation was a little less meaningful held in the impersonal gymnasium instead of in "The Hall," that ancient, red-brick building which had accommodated the smaller numbers graduating with Jamie Dewar. It was impossible to disguise this building's true function. The basketball nets swung out of the way and draped in green-and-white bunting in honor of the occasion brought to mind visions of bodies warm with sweat leaping into the air. The painted lines on the floor also emphasized the secunded function of the building, although the organizers had tried to make the space both colorful and dignified, with the raised central stage for the dignitaries, the green-and-white banners suspended from the rafters above, and the graduands' seats ringing the stage. The band, in full regalia, placed behind the graduands on the far side of the stage, faced the central aisle up which the academic procession was to march, past the audience of proud onlookers. Still it remained what it was, a decorated gymnasium.

But one shouldn't quibble. Nostalgia for *temps perdu*

was a hallmark of old age; the play's the thing, and the former ambience of "The Hall" was known only to old fogies. She smiled, reminiscing. She saw her younger self, sitting proudly on a similar stage, first in her role as a professor, later as Dean of Women, watching her own students kneeling, being hooded, and rising triumphantly to receive the accolade of a proud parent's camera flash.

The gymnasium was already almost filled. Perhaps it was as well they had come early. Now the band, muffled dissonance over, came to attention and the music of John Philip Sousa filled the air.

"Are you sure you're comfortable, Aunt Grace?" asked Andrew, beside her. She turned and nodded, smiling at him. He didn't look too comfortable himself, red hair still damp from the shower, long legs stretched under the seat in front. The chairs had not been designed for young men whose six-foot-plus height was still a source of surprise to them. She looked at him fondly and decided that she was glad, after all, that he had come with her. It would be good for him to hear Jamie Dewar. One did not frequently get the opportunity to hear an international authority expound.

Mind you, it had been a matter of principle for her to resist the family's pressure to have her go to convocation accompanied. To someone who had always been fiercely independent, a broken wrist sustained in a fall, and a stupid fall at that, was no reason to change one's way of living. Indeed, she had given in to what she considered misplaced solicitude only because she knew it was done out of love. Besides, she had a feeling Andrew might benefit from this little outing, though perhaps not in the manner the family had so arbitrarily decided. She certainly saw no need for her near and dear to hover, merely because she had returned from overseas with her arm in a cast. The frailities of age were inevitable, she knew, though the only one she feared was losing her mind. Or did one know when one had lost it? She supposed the worst was when there were short periods of lucidity, those intermittent moments of brilliant clarity when the mists parted and the old vibrant mind peeked out from the swirling fog and knew that it was doomed.

She shook herself mentally. . . . What could not be cured must be endured. Still, one wondered, for instance, if Jamie's mind would maintain itself into old age. Perhaps he would find another miracle drug: "Take twice daily to refresh your neurons."

The march ended with a flourish. A short pause, the band regrouped; then, as the echos died away, the trumpets sounded, and the crowd rose to its feet. Not a spare seat to be seen. The dignitaries in their academic robes emerged from the anonymous mass of people, like a film strip from a projector, the chaplain in the lead. Oh dear, he seemed to be in fine fettle, striding up the aisle like an avenging angel, flying robe undone, definitely unchastened. The powers that be had obviously not managed to tone him down one iota after yesterday's little fiasco, when he had enlivened an otherwise routine alumni dinner with an impromptu sermon on "Vengeance is mine, saith the Lord" in place of the expected invocation.

True, the Reverend Michael Davidson had always been a little eccentric, a trait unremarkable in an academic community. In fact, it was probably an asset, making him more noticeable to those who required his services. A servile chaplain, unobtrusive and reserved, would be lost in the mass of father figures a university provided. However, lately, he, a bachelor, had taken to addressing venerable alumni and benefactors (some actually even older than himself) as "My Children," a form of salutation not always appreciated by those to whom it was directed. When one coupled this with his recently expressed wish to be called "Father," one felt that possibly it was time for someone, though no one had yet volunteered for the honor, to point out that perhaps he was carrying eccentricity too far.

Now the procession had finished filing in. The faculty

members were all in place, multicolored hoods resplendent slashes against the somber gowns. Even Ray Clark had made an appearance. Unusual for him to be a member of the academic procession! He had eschewed all academic responsibility years ago, and was more likely to be found in the students' pub during convocation, three sheets to the wind, waving his stein exuberantly in the air and asking his students to join him in a toast to the graduates.

Yet Ray had come to convocation, albeit with his gown a little askew, his mortarboard tassle tickling his nose. Everyone else had long since given up wearing mortarboards, but then, how would Ray know that? He hadn't darkened convocation for years.

Why now? Was he making an attempt to swim up from the depths while tenure still provided an increasingly frayed safety line? Oh! Of course! Ray and Jamie had been away at Columbia together, doing their PH Ds in similar fields. Poor Ray! No wonder he was often in his cups, if he was comparing his gradual withdrawal from responsibility in any form to Jamie's meteoric rise in industry. She admired his courage in even showing up for this convocation. It must be very difficult for him to accept what his life was in comparison with what it might have been if he had only fulfilled the promise that had brought him back to Lockland.

She could see a few latecomers sidling into the reserved seats arount her. The ceremonies were about to begin.

Grace Forrester, PH D, retired Dean of Women, was a lady whom one noticed. As uncompromising now as in her youth, she yet maintained a certain naïveté about life along with an unshakable belief in the essential goodness of mankind, a faith that accorded peculiarly with an analytical, hard-headed approach to all matters scientific.

Now in her late seventies, she had won renown in her chosen field of chemistry when it had been unfashionable for women to take science and only the most determined had even gone to university. She had come to Lockland as one of the first female teachers, when it had housed only three thousand or so students, and had not only taught, but had taken it upon herself to befriend those intrepid souls who arrived to find the university ill-prepared to house them. Early on it had become evident that the women were there to stay, and, in consequence, needed somewhere to live. Soon she was busily arranging board for these emancipated souls. Eventually this task became formalized under the title "Dean of Women."

A few years before, she had retired, by choice, saying that it was time for the younger generation to take over. She proceeded, thereupon, to write three scientific books, which she said she had never previously had sufficient time to do, serve as guest lecturer all over the world, enjoy even more the nieces and nephews who comprised her family, and, generally, act as if age were just a state of mind. However, since her unfortunate fall in Venice as she was carrying her baggage out of the hotel, and which she attributed to the poor condition of the sidewalk, her family seemed determined to coddle her, a state of affairs that Grace was struggling to endure.

Those in the audience who had heard about the Reverend Mr. Davidson's lapse from grace, as one wag put it, awaited the opening ceremonies with more than usual interest. However, the chaplain, awash in an aura of official trepidation, had been constrained to give his customary invocation. J. Richardson Dewar, presented to convocation by the president, his list of achievements suitably lauded, wore the purple hood edged with gold silk reserved for LL Ds (*honoris causa*) and was now giving his falsely modest introduction to what then became a magnificent model of the rhetoric expected of one who had achieved as much in life as he so obviously had.

Grace turned back to Andrew. He had listened with becoming concentration, seemingly as impressed with the great man's performance as any youth of today could be with someone from an older generation. Yes, she thought, Jamie still had the power to hold an audience, to speak as if for your benefit alone, to make those steel-blue eyes seem to be looking right at you. It was a remarkable gift. And, as he had done with the many abilities the gods had given him, he made the most of it.

Now the graduates were moving up, two by two, to be hooded. She recognized many of the names. In some cases, she had taught their parents, others she had met at the Sunday-night suppers that were a tradition at her home, and still others' exploits she had read about in the weekly university paper. Now the official ceremonies were almost over, the awards being given. The crowd was shifting restively, eager to be out in the cool, afternoon light, their particular reasons for being there already suitably decorated for their academic achievements. The closing benediction was mercifully short, and then the band eagerly struck up the recessional.

There went the university officials: the Chancellor, enveloped in his ceremonial moirés and silks; the President, dignified and unapproachable; the Honorary Graduand, resplendent in gold and purple; the Rector; the Dean of Women; the Chaplain, eyes downcast, obviously in his humble but overwhelmed, servant-of-God mood; the Trustees, one of whom, tall and elegant, pale from the heat, swayed as she left; the academic staff; and finally the graduates, released from constraints of decorum at the exit like puppies from a leash.

"Aunt Grace, look at old Ray Clark," whispered Andrew. "He must have had a bottle with him!"

And, indeed, Ray Clark was coming out behind the graduates, being held firmly up by the elbow by an embarrassed colleague walking beside him.

"What a son of a bitch your precious new LL D is!" Grace heard him mutter to the man with him as they went by her.

"Poor man!" said Grace to Andrew. "Ray was a very bright man in his time. It's hard for him. He was a contemporary of Dr. Dewar's, you know. Perhaps he's just a little upset today."

"Nah!" replied Andrew. "This performance isn't unusual. I've seen it before. Professor Clark works in our department, you know. He comes in and asks us what we're doing. Before we get to say anything he starts telling us about how he almost was famous, but someone stole his patent. He's a really delusional drunk! He's still teaching a fourth-year class and he's usually pissed — sorry, Aunt Grace — bombed to the eyeballs."

Now the audience would begin to file out, the front rows first. Grace suspected she should wait till the crush was over. She also suspected that one of the instructions Andrew had been given was to ensure she did just that.

Really, why couldn't people file out in an orderly fashion? There was a lady in the second, left-front row, aisle seat, obstructing traffic. She seemed unwilling to leave, and equally unwilling to rise and let others go by. It was really extraordinary behavior! And some others were now gathering around her, rather than just squeezing past her. From five rows back Grace watched the small group forming concentric rings, as a pearl is formed around the grain of sand that serves as the original irritant.

CHAPTER TWO

The simile had indeed been apt. Slumped over in one of the plush seats reserved for minor dignitaries was a woman, as annoying in death as she had been irritating in life. Her name was Audrey Benedict, and technically speaking (although certainly she had never regarded convention), the dignitary in row two, left, seat one, should have been Donald Benedict, Dean of Graduate Studies. As his wife, Audrey qualified only peripherally for that seat.

Donald Benedict, a tall, spare man who had lived alone in his ivory tower until his forty-fifth year, more immune to feminine wiles than unsought, had succumbed to Cupid's dart while on a year's sabbatical. He returned, to a surprised Lockland, a married man. Soon the newlyweds forsook Don's small, shabby house near the campus, and moved into one of the newer riverlot homes on the outskirts of Marlburg. They had it "done" professionally by interior decorators from a nearby city, and filled it with ultra-modern furniture chosen from a company in the United States. Audrey Benedict had been overheard telling the local hairdresser that there were very few firms in Marlburg worth wasting one's time on.

Don and Audrey Benedict had been dutifully feted on their return by the local hostesses. Early on there were those who had vied to present those culinary masterpieces which preserved their reputations as the doyennes of Marlburg society. But Audrey Benedict, whose need for sustenance seemed miniscule, arbitrarily pushed her food around her plate, Minton or Royal Doulton notwithstanding, and then, halfway through dinner, quietly lighted up one of her special, imported, small cigars.

Twice a year, in return, the Benedicts held large, impersonal cocktail parties at the local faculty club. Here she and Don formed an uncomfortable receiving line of two, during which she dutifully extended her freckled, pale, right hand, with its long, impeccably manicured fingernails, for her guests to shake. One felt that in earlier times she would have expected it to be kissed.

The university community, that nebulous amalgam of individuals, was very fond of its Dean of Graduate Studies, partly because of his pleasant nature and high intelligence, but principally because he offered them no threat. It had also been prepared to like the new Mrs. Benedict, but this proved increasingly difficult.

Not that she was unintelligent. Indeed, she had until recently been a highly successful buyer for a luxury department store in one of the major cities in Canada. Nor was she so attractive that she engendered feelings of unease among the faculty wives or overtures from the academics she met. She was, in point of fact, thirty-eight, angular, depressingly plain, with watery blue eyes and pale lashes. She would have passed unnoticed in a crowd were it not for her expensive, couturier-designed clothes and her raucous, raspy voice.

The fact was that she was unpleasant — insensitively, blindingly so. Contemptuous of the small town of which Lockland was the major resource, sublimely indifferent to the policies evolved in the university's committee rooms, she had offended, albeit impartially, each group in the area that had opened its door to her.

Don, gaunt, earnest, and affable, with a kindly wit, continued to be well liked. His major flaw seemed to be his blind eye as far as Audrey was concerned. But for his sake, for a little while, Audrey had been offered membership in many of the organizations within the university circle. Each, in turn, she succeeded in alienating.

A glaring example that still rankled among the members, perhaps because it was so recent, had been her exposé, in an impromptu column in the Marlburg *Sentinel*, of the closed annual meeting of the Faculty Wives' Association. This august body joined town to gown by dispensing charity to Marlburg's deserving needy. Audrey had somehow managed, while supposedly reporting on the group's humanitarian endeavors, to imply that its members also sat in moral judgment on the recipients.

The group's members, feeling strongly that the decision-making process whereby "deserving" was defined and qualified was not a matter for public disclosure, had waxed quite eloquent at the subsequent, specially called meeting. Needless to say, Audrey's possible membership in the Faculty Wives' Association, had, at the same meeting, evoked considerable debate. One might even substitute "heated" for "considerable."

Two days before her demise she had struck again, this time on the local radio station's "Hot Line" program, with an impassioned advocacy of abortion on demand. This was generally believed to have been directly responsible for the chaplain's unprecedented harangue, a day later, at the alumni dinner.

It was, therefore, surprising that she should have gone gentle into that good night. Yet dead she seemed to be, the pale hands hanging limply, the flesh under the long nails cyanosed. Near her stood a woman, fortyish, mousey, wearing a flowered dress with matching jacket. She had shortly before gotten up from the seat to Audrey's left, saying "Excuse me, excuse me," in rising tones, and now, still clutching her white gloves, was sobbing hysterically into her husband's handkerchief.

Most of convocation continued to leave, duty done and the prospect of good times ahead. Parents broke ranks to join their offspring milling outside on the lawns and share in their happiness. Professors hurried away to be first out of the parking lot and home.

Few were aware of the mini-drama being played out in the second row. One of the proctors hurried over from his station near the door, glancing distractedly around as if help would be forthcoming if only he looked hard enough. A security guard, perspiring in his heavy, tightly buttoned blue uniform, was on his knees beside the crumpled form now laid out in the aisle, applying mouth-to-mouth resuscitation to the blue lips, while his compatriot leaned rhythmically with the heel of his hand on the bright yellow fabric covering Audrey's motionless chest.

The ashen-faced husband gathered his weeping wife protectively closer, blocking her view with his chest, while the band, eyes on their conductor, continued to play a sprightly medley from Gilbert and Sullivan's *Mikado*. Five rows back, Grace Forrester said quietly, "Andrew, perhaps if you slip out that side door you could call the ambulance."

CHAPTER THREE

Vanessa looked up from where she knelt on the kitchen linoleum, bent over some stiff cardboard, painting placards, to answer Ray's "Hi, 'Nessa" as he sidled in the door after convocation. He was still drunk, but not as drunk as he had been earlier in the week. By Friday he had been as drunk as she had ever known him to be during his fifteen years of intermittent bouts with the bottle. Something from his past must have precipitated this latest episode that was more real than faked.

She always knew when he was trying to live up to the image he had created for himself as Lockland's tenured sot, taunting the administration to force him to reform. This was not one of those occasions.

She thought that by now she should have been able to detach herself from the situation, to watch objectively Ray's self-destructive ploys staged gratuitously for officials he despised, as he proved to himself once again that they were too cowardly to take action. But she never could. Her emotions clouded her insight every time.

That insight had come slowly over time, during years of a marriage that had started with unreal expectations on both sides and had survived the unexpected tedium of "getting established" and many small children. But with it came a frustration that was forcing Vanessa outside of her home to find self-fulfillment.

Vanessa had always had a need to feel special, a need to live up to the uniqueness of her name. Her German immigrant parents had considered "Vanessa" an archetypically British name. It was as if by so naming her they had dubbed her, conferring all the rights and privileges that go with being born Canadian.

They had also endowed her with their desire to succeed, within the limited sphere of their experience and culture. She could hear her father saying proudly in his gruff voice, "See, Erna, vot a gut job our Vanessa iss doing with her papers! You will the Grade Twelve finish and a very gut secretary be, if you vork hard like dis!"

Occasionally Vanessa had thought she would like to be part of the academic stream going on to university, but she was realistic. She knew that her parents were saving their money to send her younger brother. She also knew that, for a girl, she was fortunate. Her two older sisters had had to quit school when they were much younger than she. Perhaps because they had never been interested in schoolwork.

The oldest had got a job in the city five-and-dime until she married at eighteen. Vanessa did not see much of Hilda, for she and her husband were very busy. Hilda drove a school bus on a rural route, and her husband was a mechanic close to the small village where Vanessa had grown up.

The second sister had married a trucker and had moved out of province. She and Vanessa still exchanged Christmas cards.

Her brother had joined the Armed Forces, uninterested in pursuing the academic career envisaged by his parents. He was stationed in Germany. Now that was ironic, she thought. Her parents had tried so hard to Anglicize them, and Rod was now back in the country they had left.

When Vanessa graduated first in the class from her commercial course she had been offered a position as a secretary in the Chemistry department at Lockland. There she had first met Ray, a young assistant professor. She had recognized the promise in him, the quick, bright intelligence honing in on the central issue. But had she perhaps missed the incipient signs of self-loathing in him? Was she so self-deluded that she had believed she could control and protect him, achieve success through him, if he put himself into her keeping?

She no longer knew. She did know that he had not needed her. His solace came out of bottles. On occasion, there had been periods of self-doubt when she feared he was ashamed of her, but these were scattered thinly between the periods of rage and frustration when she hated what he was doing to them.

Lately she had thought that she was finally accepting him for what he was: a man at war with the person he loved best — himself. Unable to vanquish his demons, she concentrated on her duties as departmental executive assistant. She had recognized that there might come a time when she would again be a single wage-earner; but she would be faithful to the last, and that would be Ray's punishment.

Vanessa had once thought she would achieve greatness by Ray's side and had fought valiantly for him. That seemed a long time ago.

Now her considerable forces were marshalled on a different front. She had become a "voice" in her own right. Ever since abortion had become legal in Canada, she had waged a determined battle to save the unborn. It became her self-appointed duty to speak for the unique fetus with its immortal soul, being destroyed in ever-increasing numbers in Marlburg.

Audrey Benedict's latest radio outburst had galvanized her into action. At first she had listened with disdain to Audrey's opening gambit in defence of abortion on demand, but when Audrey had made a call-to-arms on behalf of the cause, Vanessa had rallied her own forces.

She had arranged a protest march for outside the hospital on the holiday Monday. Her co-combatants were ready, and the weekend was to be spent preparing the placards they would carry as they slowly marched back and forth outside the hospital entrance.

Several finished placards were already leaning against

the kitchen walls to dry when she had abstractedly watched Ray drag his gown over his suit jacket, prior to attending convocation. She had set down her large pot of poster paint to help him find his hood, after he had already frantically searched through a variety of drawers. Normally, she would have immediately gone to his aid, but she had found it hard to believe that he actually intended to go to the ceremony. She felt it was unfair of him to choose this year to attend convocation.

Unlike a few years ago, she had not tried to stop him from going or searched his pockets for the hidden "mickey" she feared to find. Since her advocacy for the unborn had begun, her policy had been to leave Ray alone. Her concern was now with those who could not help themselves. Ray would have to sink or swim.

Surprisingly, and she had noticed this with detachment whenever she thought about her situation at all, he had swum, finally convinced that he was not going to drown. Whenever he was near authority, he still pretended to be caught in the undertow, but the demons that pulled him under came less frequently, and he often floated, becalmed.

He had returned late from convocation, gown off one shoulder, stumbling slightly, long after she was safely back home, putting the finishing touches on her placards. He had an ironic glint in his eye that she, looking up from the drops of blood she was drawing, recognized as meaning he had something to say that involved her. She knew he wanted her to question him, but she wasn't about to give him the satisfaction. She bent back to her work, dipping her brush into the blood-red paint, wiping the excess carefully off on the rim of the jar.

"I don't think you'll be needing your placards, 'Nessa," he said contentedly, his speech slurred.

Her head jerked up. She stared at him fixedly. What did he know? Why this year, of all years, had he felt the need to go to convocation? Why did he always manage to give her a fresh worry?

"What do you mean, Ray?" she asked. She watched him trying to get his gown off, the hood around his neck obstructing him.

"Your little broadcaster failed to make it out of convocation. She had a heart attack or something."

"Ray, no! Are you sure? How do you know?"

"She was out cold in the aisle when the people got up to leave."

"She probably just fainted, Ray. It gets so hot in there."

"Really, doctor? Then why did they take her away to the hospital in an ambulance with a blanket covering her face?"

She reared back as if struck.

"She can't be! You must be wrong! You must have been dr . . ."

Her voice screeched to a stop. She had never mentioned his drunkenness directly to him. She always just tried harder to work around his disability.

"You mean I must have been drunk. Is that what you almost said, 'Nessa?" he asked politely. "Finally been able to say the word? Drunk, 'Nessa, d-r-u-n-k. No, I watched what was going on very carefully. She was blue, and she was quiet for once, and she was taken away with her face covered."

He leered at her and swayed slightly.

Vanessa got up, brushed off her knees, rubbed her lower back, and started distractedly for the door. Her husband anticipated her.

"I've already got the paper," he said, waving it tantalizingly in front of her nose. "They haven't got anything in about Audrey Benedict yet. Only the usual blurb on the famous speakers they're supposed to have at convocation today. They do promise you a complete account in Tuesday's edition of the *Sentinel*. If you can't wait till then, you'll have to try your tom-toms to get the news, 'Nessa."

He smirked.

Vanessa snatched the paper from him and leafed through it hurriedly. Ray was right. The paper would have gone to press before the ceremony began. Suddenly she stopped and thought. Was that why Mrs. Benedict had not come back out? She must have been already dead!

"Why did you go to convocation, Ray?" she asked slowly, consideringly. "You haven't gone for years. It wasn't because Audrey Benedict was likely to be there, was it?"

"You're right again, my beloved," he commented approvingly. "The mentality of the sign-painter has not yet completely erased the astuteness that I once cherished. No, it was our charming guest speaker who has, somehow, irrevocably captured what I am pleased to call my imagination. I felt this inexplicable need to watch Jamie Dewar receive the plaudits of the crowd," and he pirouetted inanely in front of Vanessa.

"But why did you want to watch him?" she asked, bewildered. "You've got nothing to do with the guest speaker. You didn't graduate from Lockland, and he left here long before you came on staff."

"Wrong, fair lady," smiled Ray, tripping over his gown as he went to put it on the kitchen table, "wrong for once. I knew Jamie Dewar when we were both at Columbia."

His slightly bloodshot eyes grew hard. "He's the bastard who stole my invention, patented it, and made a fortune from it! Oh, God damn it! If I'd only found out then! If she'd warned me then, so I could have stopped him! It isn't fair that he gets all the credit! He's living in luxury and I'm. . . ." He looked with loathing at the placards drying near him and aimed an uncertain kick at one.

Vanessa had heard Ray in his cups before, whining about having lost out on success and fame, but never before had he been specific in his complaints. She wondered if he could be telling the truth. His next remarks stopped her in her tracks.

"I knew your baby-killer at Columbia, too," he said. "Only she was Audrey Follows, then. Just a little undergraduate, starting her distinguished career."

CHAPTER FOUR

"I'm thinking of running for office, Daniel," Stanley, the older man standing on one side of the autopsy table, declared facetiously to his chief resident. "My campaign platform will be to ban Sunday post-mortems. My slogan will be: 'If you're really dead on Sunday, we guarantee to keep you that way until Monday.' Interested in voting for me?"

He cast a sidelong glance at the coroner, who, materializing periodically in the doorway like an unanchored metronome at its apogee, wandered up and down the outside corridor, and said wryly: "Spent yesterday attending convocation! Now this! Even the Lord rested on the seventh day! However, the little lady continues to have power, dead or alive!" He gesticulated with his scalpel towards the stainless-steel table on which a body was lying.

The speaker was a distinguished-looking man in his early fifties, of middle height, with thick gray hair, and blue eyes that often crinkled with laughter. He had a sense of dedication that he took inordinate pains to conceal, and had, in actual fact, placed his name on the weekend-duty roster so that his staff could enjoy the holiday. And just as well, it turned out, with a colleague's wife as subject!

Daniel Stein, the chief resident, had worked for the Chief for four years and knew him well. He, therefore, accepted the token protest for what it was.

"Since it's just a routine coroner's case to ascertain the cause of death, we'll get it done in no time!" he said, cheerfully. "Never you worry, sir! Once we haul out the heart and show the infarct . . . we could practically close up, then and there. I suppose no one expects a woman of her age to have a myocardial infarct," he went on conversationally. "Too bad she had to pick the middle of convocation to do it in!".

It was Stein's last weekend on call. His final examinations loomed a month away, and he figured that the two of them could finish the autopsy within two hours and then he could get back to the books, those interminable books that his wife threatened to burn the day after he took his examinations.

"You have to be very old and unwanted to find a convenient time to die, Dan," replied the Chief. "It's been my experience that otherwise you generally bother someone on your way out. You know," he went on meditatively, "the coroner would certainly prefer this to be an infarct. But he can't get a history of heart trouble, and her poor, devastated husband swears she's never been ill." He peered over his half-glasses towards the open door and called to the morgue attendant, "Let's get on with it, Charlie."

From the hallway came the shuffle of feet, and a small, rotund creature, with nicotine-stained hands and wearing a clear plastic apron over "greens," appeared in the doorway.

"Keep your shirt on, Doc," said the apparition. "The Old Doc's here and him and me were just gabbing."

Ed Stanley cast his resident a resigned look. Ed had been Chief of Pathology for fifteen years, and a remarkably good one. During his tenure he had rebuilt his department to meet the exigencies of modern times. He had added expertise to the staff, gained recognition for his own considerable academic achievements, and had arranged the relocation of the department to larger quarters which provided space for young researchers and for educating budding pathologists. But one thing remained immutable: the peripatetic appearances of the Emeritus Professor, or, as he was referred to by generations of staff and residents, the "Old Doc."

The "Old Doc" had a nose for trouble, and he exploited it. It was commonly believed that if you pulled a corpse from the river, the "Old Doc" would be standing on the bridge watching. And if you diagnosed, then lost the patient to the first case of "Mojo's Syndrome" the world had ever known, the "Old Doc" would materialize beside the autopsy table as the initial incision was being made.

To the uninitiated, he seemed only to be a funny old man, careless of his appearance, always wearing the same blue suit with the baggy knees and the striped tie with the inevitable cigarette burn. Many the young, eager new resident had thought him past his prime. But although he was elderly, his gait slow and careful, the rheumy brown eyes in his lined, leathery face were still keen. Experience had added to, not replaced, his intelligence.

Daniel could remember back four years to his own first reaction to the "Old Doc." Now he knew exactly what Ed Stanley's look of resignation meant. It was directed to what "Old Doc's" arrival signified, not at the old man himself. "Look out, here comes trouble," said the look. "Good-bye, simple coronary occlusion. Hello, hara-kari."

Charlie flicked on the overhead lights above the stainless-steel table on which the naked body of Audrey Benedict rested, the arms limp, the long, pale fingers barely curled. The "Old Doc" meandered over to the two banked rows of metal seats generally reserved for medical students, snapped one down, and settled himself comfortably.

"Better take a good look at her back," said the Emeritus Professor to his successor, not so much in an admonishing way but as if sharing in an interesting moment. He sagely nodded his leonine head and leaned slightly forward. The show that always interested him most was about to begin.

However, when they turned the corpse to rest face down, the back that they exposed was unremarkable. Certainly the usual signs of *livor mortis* were there, discoloring the freckled skin. She had, after all, lain supine overnight on the shelf in the morgue refrigerator. There was no stab wound, no fractured cervical vertebrae, no deformity of any kind. Only in the deltoid region of her right arm was there the slightest peculiarity: a small, round puncture that a less astute pathologist might very well have missed. But there were some added clues to guide him: a drop of dried blood on her upper arm that mirrored the one found on the sleeve of her bright yellow dress, less than the expected degree of rigor mortis, and the presence of the "Old Doc."

The old man stayed for most of the post-mortem. He listened as they dictated into the overhead microphone, beginning with a description of "the body of a middle-aged Caucasian female, 163 cms.," through "the standard Y-shaped incision exposing the internal organs," to the findings of the expected *petechiae* or pinpoint bruises overlying the lungs and heart. He departed without comment as the conclusion — "generalized anoxic changes but no definitive cause of death" — was dictated to close out the summary.

The coroner had wandered into the room to watch as they excised the block of tissue around the puncture site and labeled the bottles that contained the various body fluids and tissues that a suspicious death required to be analyzed. He cast a quizzical glance at the Chief of Pathology but said nothing. The little bottles were saying it all.

Ed Stanley had not known Audrey Benedict nearly as well in life as he did now in death, but one thing he was sure of: She would have hated this. Not the inescapable fact that she was naked (she might, on occasion, have flaunted that), but the objective exposure of her biological being, the impersonal probing of the scalpel into her limp flesh, the deliberate, detailed sorting and bottling of her body fluids. It would have been the science she objected to, she who had always controlled others by her arts.

"I swear to you that sometimes I think the old boy does them in himself," a disgruntled Dan Stein muttered to the retreating back of the Emeritus Professor, as he screwed the lid onto the last specimen jar labeled "Forensic Laboratory." Lunchtime was long past, and little of the afternoon remained for studying.

"He'd be a multiple murderer then, Dan," said Ed Stanley philosophically. "The guy's been picking them out for close to fifty years."

CHAPTER FIVE

From his vantage point in a large, overstuffed chair next to the fireplace, Andrew surveyed the group in his great-aunt's living room. He had been abstractedly watching Penny, his girlfriend. Crouched on a hassock, her long, dark hair swirling to her shoulders, she was animatedly joining in the discussion. How unlike the stereotyped picture of the female medical student this tiny, elfin girl was, he thought yet again. He was content to sit quietly and watch how she became a vital part of whatever group she found herself in . . . not by pushing her opinions on people, but by listening and, somehow, understanding. It was one of the reasons he loved her so.

His eyes surveyed the room. It was the usual, unlikely group that made Aunt Grace's Sunday-night suppers so interesting. He noted lazily some old friends of his great-aunt's, an occasional erudite professor, some young students from various disciplines; the variety always ensured fascinating discussions on unusual topics. He knew the young were supposed to be contemptuous of tradition — and when Aunt Grace was in town, these Sunday-night suppers were definitely a tradition — but he loved these gatherings.

However, there was something askew, something a little out of whack. He wondered about it. The group was the usual unusual assortment. The food was the standard fare that Sarah, Grace's housekeeper of many years' standing, always provided. No surprises there. Just ample amounts of turkey, ham, scalloped potatoes, buns, salad. . . . The room, with its old-fashioned dusty blue velvet drapes closed against the night, its sofas and chairs covered with faded chintz, its Victorian whatnots, and its lamps making soft pools of light, remained the same.

The difference was there, though. Intangible, tantalizing, like a thought only half-formed. And so he pursued it, lazily listening to the conversations as they swirled and eddied around him. Suddenly it came to him. They were all talking about the same subject! Although the invitations had been made long before the weekend now ending, although the guests came from varying walks of life and were bound together only by the string of Grace's interest, although they spoke in separate groups, they were all talking about Audrey Benedict, her life, her relationships, and, most of all, her unexpected death.

He could, by concentrating, pull a snatch of conversation from the general maelstrom. He honed in on Bob Saunders'. An undergraduate, and fellow student of Andrew's, you would think his contact with the wife of the Dean of Graduate Studies would be limited, yet here he was saying that he must have been one of the last people to see her alive.

Andrew struggled up from the recesses of his chair to demand: "How could you have been? You were playing in the band for a good hour before convocation started. She didn't even come in until the procession was seated! You mean you saw her come in late? What's special about that? She was in full view of everybody else!"

"Well, it was a little more involved than that," admitted Bob. "There's a long segment in one of the marches where I don't play, so I sort of perfected this scheme for getting out for a cigarette." He ignored the incredulous look on Andrew's face and went on. "There's only the one bit for me right at the very beginning, and so after it, I took off. It was really getting hot up there. Anyway, I went out to the lobby for a cigarette, and there she was, wearing dark sunglasses, Miss Cool herself! She was leaning against the far wall, nose in the air as usual, wearing this bright yellow dress, obviously looking for somebody. She seemed sort of anxious. But I figure she knew, if the person she was waiting for didn't come mighty soon, she was going to have to walk in late."

"Boy, old Lizard Lips would have had a stroke if he knew you'd taken off during a performance," said Andrew, momentarily diverted by the heresy of Bob's actually leaving the stage. "And you know his views on a musician smoking!"

"Well, he's opinionated. I think he and Mrs. Benedict would make a good couple," replied Bob, thereby managing the feat of combining irreverence for his hard-working conductor with a sublime disregard for the events of the past twenty-four hours.

Elsewhere the conversation was more serious. "You feel so helpless!" Daphne Forrester, Andrew's mother, was explaining. "Don's devastated! He's sitting at home in that huge, impersonal house, staring at those ghastly abstracts on the wall, and I don't think he's moved from his chair all day. If I only knew what we could do to help him."

"I went over earlier today," volunteered an elderly lady with iron-gray hair blunt cut around a face devoid of make-up. "I told him he could move into one of my spare rooms for a while if he wanted to get away. You remember he stayed with me when he first came to Marlburg? But you're right! He isn't capable right now of making any decisions. He just sits. So I sat with him until his sister, Milly, and her husband arrived from Denham. At least enough people are bringing food to the house so that they won't have to worry about that. I thought I'd pop back in tomorrow to see what needs doing."

Andrew smiled fondly at the lady who'd just spoken. She was his aunt's oldest friend, Margaret McDuff by name, the last surviving member of the founding family of Marlburg. Her ancestors had founded the town, had owned much of it, run most of it, and now dominated in perpetuity the nearby cemetery, lying decently interred beneath the largest, most hideous marble monument that a Victorian McDuff had been able to commission.

Margaret had not been permitted to go to university in her youth, but had been required to "come out," in accepted McDuff tradition. At her "coming-out" ball she had met a charming man of whom her parents had approved, and was engaged to be married when he contracted typhoid fever and died within the month. She had never married, nor worked outside her home, but lived on the money that had been left in trust for her by her father, doled out by the bank her father had chosen. She remained the sole McDuff in the family home which she had inherited.

Surprisingly, her life had not been useless. Combining intelligence with a warm heart, she took in strays and foundlings, both canine and human, with complete indifference to what was expected of her by heritage and her neighbors.

Her huge home had housed a variety of characters over the years, but only one became a permanent fixture. The university chaplain had moved in temporarily thirty years before until he "found a place." It remained a credit to both their characters that never a breath of scandal touched their relationship. She fed him and cared for him, while they carried on a continuous debate about the deeper aspects of earthly existence, the social responsibilities of human beings (their concepts varied widely), and religion.

It might have seemed surprising that religion could be a source for debate, for Margaret McDuff had been staunchly Presbyterian from birth, but somehow, over the years, her faith had become tinged with agnosticism. The chaplain, meanwhile, veered more and more to the outward manifestations of religious conviction. She had steered him off the idea of incense in the university's non-denominational chapel only recently. It was said that Margaret McDuff, singular as she was, was the ballast that kept the Reverend Mr. Davidson's balloon from soaring into the stratosphere.

"The big problem," she went on, "is the funeral. I don't think that Don has really grasped the fact that Audrey is dead. He's in such a state of shock that he's not thinking straight."

"What do you mean, Margaret?" asked Daphne.

"Oh, he's demanding that she have all the honors that are due her, whatever they are. He's acting as if everybody thought she was wonderful. He seems to have total amnesia about all the controversy she's stirred up recently. He as much as told me he expects a huge ceremonial university service!"

"The only people who'll go are the people who don't want Don to be hurt. Except, of course, for all those individuals who will go to hear whatever exciting things the chaplain chooses to come out with!" said Daphne, summing up the problem succinctly.

"Exactly!" agreed Margaret. "Now I ask you, what happens if in the middle of the service, the university chaplain launches into a tirade against the deceased?" She stared intently at her audience, worriedly gauging their reactions.

"Margaret, you know he's not going to do anything like that," replied Grace, soothingly. "He's incapable of hurting another human being. He must have been extremely provoked to talk like that at the alumni dinner. And he didn't even direct his remarks at anybody then."

"Something Don said today made me wonder if he thinks that Audrey was upset by someone recently. He was talking about vindication. Then more people came in and he seemed to relapse back into silence," volunteered Daphne.

"There's talk that it wasn't a heart attack," said a tall, middle-aged man sitting quietly on the other side of the fireplace. Andrew knew him as a Classics professor, and although he did not know him well, knew that he was considered worth listening to.

"They say that she's not being buried for a while," he continued. "Rumor has it that the coroner has called in the police."

The voices suddenly stilled. All eyes focused on the speaker till Margaret, ever forthright, leaned forward towards him and said into the silence, "Whatever do you mean?"

The Classics professor explained softly, "You can't bury anyone until the cause of death is known, and they don't know it yet. The pathologists have sent specimens to the Forensic Laboratory to help them determine the cause of death, and that takes a while." He shrugged. "So it's likely immaterial to speculate on what our good chaplain is going to say at the funeral for a while yet."

CHAPTER SIX

J. Richardson Dewar was uncomfortable. This was a novel sensation for him, and all the more acute as he was unaccustomed to it.

He sat on the straight wooden chair on the rickety front porch of the family homestead, in the place of honor, while relations and neighbors vied to speak to him. The location, no, the very chair, brought back memories of his existence in that bleak house with his widowed, silent, disapproving father. If he went up the narrow back stairs to that small, back bedroom with its peeling wallpaper, he knew he would find the same pocked iron bedstead, lumpy mattress, small splintered desk with the gooseneck lamp, where he had done his homework late at night after the chores were done.

But it was not his adolescent ghost that made him twine his feet around the legs of the chair. Nor was it because he was unused to gatherings held in his honor. Indeed, he had come to regard them as his due. He felt no sense of pride or even justification that these simple country folk from whom he stemmed should suddenly be so eager to please. Nor did he feel contrition for the silent years, now past. These people mattered not at all to him.

His sense of unease sprang from a deeper well. It niggled and nagged at him, occupying the forefront of his mind as he dealt mechanically with the civilities expected of him.

Why, oh why, had he been fool enough to take up with Audrey again? She had caught him in an off-guard moment just as the speeches ended. He had noticed a very elegant trustee's wife surreptitiously eying him and had been considering going over to talk to her when suddenly, there was Audrey. He should have ignored her . . . pretended not to recognize her. It might have worked. But on the other hand, it had always been dangerous to snub Audrey. She used to make that very clear.

There had been very little time in which to analyze the situation. How could he possibly have anticipated that one of his former lovers would turn up as the wife of a stuffy dean in this obscure backwater? Especially in the old home town which he had abandoned long before he knew her? She had insisted that he meet her Saturday morning. Now that she was dead, God alone knew what old coals the town would be raking over. Meanwhile he was locked into a family reunion, condemned to remain until at least Wednesday.

It had been funny to see old Clarkie reeling up the aisle. Amazing that Lockland still kept him on. Thank heavens he himself hadn't been stupid enough to opt for a safe academic career instead of going for the real world. . . .

He brushed the recalcitrant lock of brown hair off his forehead again and smiled at Aunt Agnes. Or was the silly woman mouthing gentilities at his Cousin Mildred? What did he care about somebody's grandchildren, or his dead father, rot his soul? Oh, for this interminable day to end! If he could have left Marlburg on the Sunday, been safely away before the gossips started in. But he had agreed to this Dewar reunion and celebration weeks before, when the Dewars had first found out that he was being honored by the university. It would look peculiar if he left now. He had too much to lose! Could he pretend to be ill? He felt ill, God knew; he was sweaty and weak in the knees, and very, very panicky.

His mind kept going back to Audrey. What had he ever

seen in her? She had never been beautiful. Today a primary requirement for his women was that they be beautiful, do him justice. It was difficult now to explain the outburst of passion that had consumed him during those callow days at graduate school. She had seemed so . . . essential, then.

But passion was a fruit that had become overripe with time. His jaded palate responded now only to the tart, tangy taste of immediacy. He could hardly recall the emotion he had felt for Ruth, the one woman he'd married, or Susan, or that pretty but dumb blonde at Yale when he was lecturing, or that married girl in the lab. Marilyn? The name eluded him. Her husband had been rather unpleasant. That he did remember! He realized it was his fate to become involved with women who would, in time, bore him. None of them measured up to his capabilities. As he inevitably grew in stature they faded into obscurity, and it was probably a kindness to let them go.

Audrey, at least, had not clung. She had been one of his early women, and at the time of that final episode she was already interested in someone else. Or so she had said. She had been very eager to see him again! He had believed it was his status as convocation speaker, rising high above the stagnant pool of academics she normally dealt with. Audrey had always believed in prestige by association. His fear of guilt by association had forced him to agree to meet her secretly, hard as it had been to disappear Saturday morning. But once he had publicly recognized her, the die was cast.

At least she was intelligent. Thank God she had wanted to avoid being seen as much as he. They had agreed to meet in the maze in the Hampton Court garden (gift of the history class of '52). Surely no one had seen them there! It was just a case of surviving this never-ending reception, this opening salvo in the Dewar Reunion, the pot-luck supper, the rhubarb pies ("You always loved rhubarb pie, Jamie"). When had they ever before cared what he liked? And then he would make his excuses and go back to Montreal.

Perhaps he would go to the chalet in the Laurentians. He deserved a holiday, and he could postpone that trip to Spain for a week or so. Plead fatigue. No, that could be interpreted as weakness, and in his business, if the wolves smelled weakness, they gathered.

Jack Mitchell was very obviously a young wolf, snapping at Jamie's professional heels. Ever since Head Office had sent in the General to apply army methods, army discipline, to the running of the Canadian operation, Jamie had been aware of the need to be very circumspect. The General might as well have belonged to the Salvation Army, for all the righteous morality he was foisting on his employees.

"My boy!" he'd said to Jamie, slapping him heartily on the back. "This company has always gone far because we recognize that God rewards those who work hard and do His bidding. Capitalism succeeds because communism is godless!"

So, perhaps it would be better to go to Spain, carry on as usual. Maybe, being out of the country legitimately was a good plan. Or would he be asked to assist the police in their inquiries? Is that what one did in Canada? Perhaps he had read too many British murder mysteries. Need they ever know that he had known Audrey Benedict in the past? Had she talked? Oh God, who was this hideous small boy being pushed towards him whom they expected him to recognize and admire?

He could hear one of the aunts behind him explaining ". . . head of research in a big drug company, all over the world." This to a little old neighbor lady, hair in a wispy gray bun, dutifully leaning over so as to hear more clearly what miracles a Dewar relative had achieved.

He stood up and began to stroll around the porch to avoid the rest of the neighbors queuing up to be introduced. Let them look at him instead: Dewar boy made good.

He was under no illusions. His relatives had paid no attention to him until he had become famous. If they had remembered him at all it had been as Fred's son, who up and left after he got so uppity and went to university and all. But all Dewars were proud, vaingloriously proud. Any prodigal son of theirs would have been righteously ignored; but a successful son merited a family reunion, provided there were neighbors there to witness it.

He knew too that he was something to see. He knew how well his deceptively simply tailored suit set off his trim body, kept fit with squash or tennis three times a week. Let them note the gold Rolex, the signet ring with the Dewar crest on the little finger of his left hand. No roughened, dirt-engrained hands for this Dewar! The striped shirt with the monogram, handmade in Hong Kong, the silk tie; they were all part of J. Richardson Dewar, world-renowned research chemist and inventor. Only the lank brown forelock refused to fit the image that Jamie Dewar had constructed over the years.

He smiled at a little girl who was paying him no attention and strolled over to the edge of the porch to pat her on the head. Jamie Dewar did not like being ignored.

CHAPTER SEVEN

The woman who had tried to move past Audrey Benedict's slumped form as convocation ended had not fully recovered from the shock. Her husband, usually ineffectual, had taken charge, driving her home as soon as the ambulance had removed Audrey's corpse and they were allowed to leave. She could not compose herself enough to go to the reception after convocation.

Her husband had tried to comfort her, a task rendered difficult by the fact that for years Helen and Ted Clay had coexisted for the sake of their children, the circles of their lives touching only in the intersecting arc of a conventional marriage. But Helen was past comforting. She wept and shuddered, and stiffened alarmingly whenever she was approached.

It became a long, dark, histrionic night, in which Ted had their family doctor around twice. The first time, sympathetic, he had given her a sleeping pill, a loving pat on the shoulder, and an admonition that he knew she would feel better in the morning. But Helen could not gag down the little gelatine capsule. His second house call, made three hours later, was to inject her with a sedative. This time he was more brusque and impersonal, and addressed his advice to Ted, muttering baleful instructions on how often he could administer the little yellow Valium tablets.

Throughout the morning, Ted doled out the tablets as

often as he dared, served them with cups of tea, which were all Helen could force down, and cautioned the children, marooned on an island of uncertainty, to be very quiet around their mother. He had even forsaken his beloved garden to minister to her needs.

As a botanist, Ted felt that May was the most important month to work in a garden. He never acknowledged, on a conscious level, that his garden was his compensation for his failures elsewhere. He wondered idly if Helen had realized that he had not been promoted yet again.

What rankled him particularly was his students' indifference to "The Popular Botanist," the new course he had designed, and the knowledge that he had lost the "Best Garden Award" to the Benedicts last year because Audrey had imported a landscape artist whom she claimed had just confirmed her own designs.

Another emerging disappointment was the increasing surliness of his son Paul, outrageously spoiled by Helen. Also, and he was surprised to note that it still had the power to hurt, the fact that Helen, so ambitious for him, was ashamed of him.

Only in his garden, walled in by greenery, among the beds of spiky iris, huge nodding poppies, and heavy-headed peonies, with his prize roses just over their winter's hibernation, did Ted Clay feel a success.

However, on that warm Sunday, when the spring grass was newly green and lush, when he had flats of annual bedding plants waiting to be tucked into the sun-warmed soil and the perennials to be protected as they came up, in short, when the most important weekend of the committed gardener was at hand, Ted found himself inside his house.

Helen had lain prostrate on their bed, her face swollen and distorted, sunk in such inner misery that all his tentative ministrations went unnoticed. He had found nothing that would comfort her and free him. But leave her he could not. Not out of an atavistic sense of compassion, but because he had no idea of what she might do. The sluggish trickle of her apathy could change without warning into a rampaging torrent of hysteria, as when she had suddenly struggled upright and, howling, had swept the lamp on the bedside table onto the floor. It had taken him some time to sweep up the shards, eyeing her guardedly as she lay there again, uncaring.

By Monday afternoon Ted, normally so unassuming and reticent, was, in his own way, desperate. His organized wife, usually so dependable, while quieter than on Sunday, had become an unpredictable creature. He spared a thought for his daughters, vanished God knows where. The house, usually a model of efficiency, had become chaotic. He had never had to keep house before. Where could he get help? Helen's mother had died six months before; his own mother was in a nursing home a province away.

He looked around the bedroom. The dirty clothes on the floor, the sticky dishes on the tray, the overflowing waste-paper basket. He shuddered at the thought of the havoc that reigned in the kitchen. He looked back at his wife, whom he dared not leave. From the depths of his desperation he telephoned Margaret McDuff, who came resignedly to deal with Helen, while Ted thankfully escaped to his garden.

Margaret looked at Helen, lying beached in what the real-estate agent had described as "the master bedroom, ensuite" when the Clays had bought the unpretentious bungalow, their "starter" home. Another crying spell was beginning. Helen's shoulders heaved with great, convulsive sobs; the salt tears coursed down the familiar tracks on her puffy cheeks; her eyes were swollen and red. The bizarre speech was being forced again and again past the trembling lips, like a roller towel unfurling, in staccato bursts, its dirty linen.

"And then I turned to her politely and said 'Excuse me,' and she wouldn't move. She — wouldn't move! My leg touched her knee, and . . . and . . . and then I saw that she was all curled over in her seat. The men came over and they tried, but they couldn't revive her. She was dead. Dead beside me. I can't bear it!"

Margaret made soothing noises while the stuttered litany of death continued to roll. It occurred to Margaret that Helen's reaction was out of proportion to the scene being so repetitiously described. Her eyes narrowed and, as so often happened, her mind began to view the scene in front of her analytically.

It was ironic, indeed, that the two women had been seated next to each other. It was common knowledge to all and sundry, including Margaret, that Audrey Benedict and Helen Clay did not speak. It had been a chance remark of Audrey's, sotto voce, in the days when she was being courted by the faculty wives, that had caused the vote for president to swing away from Helen. The softly spoken barb had reduced to rubble Helen's towering aspirations. Since that time, Helen had secretly ascribed every ill at her own door to the malicious intervention of Audrey Benedict.

Hidden deep within the secret soul of Helen Clay was the conviction that it had been Audrey's influence that had caused Don Benedict to veto Ted's advancement. She felt that in the seclusion of the Benedict's home Audrey gloated over Ted's failure to make full professor, yet again. Oh yes, Helen had known for two weeks that the letters of promotion were out. If not, Ted's silence had been clue enough. He had been by-passed again.

Since the day that Audrey Benedict had declined membership in the Faculty Wives' Association with the feeble excuse that she, who did not work, was too busy, Helen had taken personally every slight and innuendo cast at the association. The Faculty Wives' was her cause, as Ted's garden was his. It gave her stature in the community, a reserved seat at convocation, a sense of worth outside her home. It compensated her for Ted's shortcomings.

If she could have attributed Paul's possible involvement with drugs, a suspicion that she still was unable to accept, to Audrey's malign influence, she would have done so. She had often wondered about the moral fiber of a woman who would smoke cigars.

It was therefore with a slight sense of disbelief that Margaret listened to the distraught woman repetitiously describe the scene at convocation.

"I know, dear," said Margaret, mustering patience, "it's an awful shock to your system. But pull yourself together, woman! Life goes on! It happened. It's over. You can't do anything about it. You just go on! Think of the children!" She waved both stubby hands determinedly, cutting the air with quick, incisive strokes.

"I can't, I can't! I touched her and she was limp!" Her teeth bit into her knuckles as the macabre little scene unwound again.

Margaret supposed that Helen must be having an attack of early "Middle-Life Syndrome" or something, not that she could ever remember having succumbed to such an ailment herself. She looked at Helen lying disheveled among the rumpled bed clothes, her blonde hair unkempt, the fair skin crepey on her neck, the utilitarian nightie crumpled and in need of washing. She had aged twenty years since convocation.

"For goodness sake, Helen, pull yourself together," she exhorted. "The children will be home soon. You don't want them to see you like this. It's not as if you and Audrey were ever close." (Understatement of the month, she thought irreverently.) "You're a nurse, you must have seen death before. Now I want you to get up and try to get going. . . ."

Margaret found it hard to imagine that Helen had ever been a nurse. Right now it was difficult to see how Helen had ever functioned as a volunteer at the Marlburg Psychiatric Hospital. Yet it was well known that Helen had single-handedly organized a volunteer corps there from the ranks of the Faculty Wives'. This type of charitable contribution was expected of a woman who truly aspired to become an executive of the association.

Margaret could not help feeling that at the present

moment Helen would have been indistinguishable from the inmates. But then, it often was hard to tell the players without a program. That was probably why the volunteers wore short blue coats as a uniform.

Finally Margaret had had enough. Talking all the while, she pulled down the bedclothes, swung Helen's feet to the floor and coerced her into the adjacent bathroom. There, with Helen propped against the sink, she scrubbed the tear-stained face, then coaxed her into a skirt and blouse and forcefully propelled her down into the kitchen. Pulling out a kitchen chair, she pushed Helen into it. Suggesting astringently that she should at least portray a semblance of normalcy for the sake of the children, Margaret found a pan, potatoes, a peeler, and handed them to Helen.

Interestingly enough, Margaret's astringency became the solution for Helen's hysteria. Unreached by Ted's solicitude or the doctor's panaceas, Helen found Margaret's matter-of-fact approach to be the needed goad.

Looking around a short while later at the tidy kitchen, the meal underway, Margaret gave qualified approval. "That's better!" she said. Helen gave Margaret a tentative smile.

"Thank you!" she said tremulously. "I don't know what got into me!" Her lower jaw began to work, but Margaret was having none of it. She picked up a pile of laundry and handed it to Helen. She pointed to the laundry-room door. Actions always spoke louder than words for Margaret McDuff.

CHAPTER EIGHT

Margaret's absence seemed to the Reverend Michael Davidson a heaven-sent opportunity to be seized and acted upon. When she had returned late the night before from her Sunday-night outing to Grace's he had still been up, worried and concerned. They had had a long, serious talk about his responsibilities to Don Benedict. Margaret had felt quite strongly that he should wait until Don asked him formally to officiate at a university service for Audrey. She had not bothered to outline to him that her reason for advising caution was the result of his impassioned speech at the alumni dinner. She had also not mentioned the Classics professor's conjecture. Margaret never repeated hearsay.

But now Margaret was conveniently elsewhere, and it seemed to Michael Davidson that this call upon her time was God's way of saying "Follow your conscience, my man, and never mind having to justify what you know to be right to Margaret!" After all, a university chaplain had many responsibilities that a mere woman would be unable to understand. It was perhaps appropriate that women were given responsibilities in churchly matters commensurate with their native abilities.

This, too, was a contentious issue that he and Margaret had jousted over before. It seemed most peculiar that this should be such a vital issue to Margaret, for it would be hard to imagine a person more unlikely to want to enter the pulpit than Margaret. Yet, here she was, making demands for privileges that she herself would never dream of accepting. It seemed a ludicrous position for her to adopt, as he had often pointed out to her and just as often been surprised by the vehemence of her defence.

Michael Davidson was a good man. He had been brought up as a Victorian, an anachronism in the twentieth century, by elderly parents. A dearly loved addition to their old age, he had presented to his parents, as their ultimate reward for raising such a dutiful son, his entry into the Church.

As a twentieth-century Victorian he had been taught to avoid argument, to restrain undue emotion. It sometimes came painfully to him that he did indeed debate rather fiercely with Margaret. Indeed he had, if truth be known, displayed perhaps an unseemly degree of emotion at the alumni dinner. This had troubled his conscience severely, although he knew it had been done from the purest of motives. He had found it necessary to liken his attack to the hymn "Onward, Christian Soldiers, Marching as to War" before he had been able to sleep that night.

In appearance, he was a frail, ascetic man, who seemed sustained more by his inner vision than by earthly requirements, except for those material comforts that glorified the Church. When he put on his vestments, one knew that it was not his venal, fine-boned frame he was adorning, but a form used to display the outward manifestations of religious life, to the greater glory of God. He had recently grown a beard to appear more prophet-like.

As well, he came with few personal requirements. He had no hobbies. He appeared to have no vices. He existed comfortably at Margaret's in his single room. He ate what was put before him, first thanking God with an age-old prayer, and seemed to have no aspirations to rise in the Church's hierarchy. He had woven himself over the years into the university tapestry, and knew, as he knew his own soul, that God had called him to minister to that community during his earthly life. Lockland was his life, as well as his job.

And so, Michael Davidson, somberly garbed, took a taxi to the Benedicts' home. His features fell instinctively into an appropriately mournful expression, beard quivering, as he nodded respectfully to the trio walking solemnly down the front steps towards him. He recognized among them the Dean of Arts and was glad for Don that officials of the university were paying their respects on this sunny, holiday Monday.

Don's sister answered his knock, and with muted voice, welcomed him and ushered him into the living room where Don sat. Don seemed out of place in the room, which could have been lifted intact from the cover of a *Better Homes and Gardens* magazine.

The room was rectangular, with an oversized, modernistic, chiseled stone fireplace dominating the north wall, while large, floor-to-ceiling windows overlooking the river spanned the west wall. The other two walls were stark white stucco. A huge, abstract painting in shades of sapphire and azure blue looked as if it had been commissioned to complement the deep blue wall-to-wall shag carpet. A large gray, pitted sculpture of a woman's torso stood on the hearth like a truncated Venus. Stiff white leather furniture stood adamantly among pots of broad-leafed, carnivorous foliage.

Don Benedict was dwarfed by the high-backed chair in which he huddled. He seemed to have shrunk overnight, his bones closer to the surface of his body. It was a curious illusion. His sister, an older, female replica of her rawboned brother, hovered nearby with her husband, who had, after years of marriage, so taken on the appearance of a Benedict that the trio appeared to consist of two brothers and a sister.

There was silence as the Reverend Mr. Davidson began his heartfelt expressions of sympathy. Don Benedict stared at the rug, his eyes veiled, his body slumped, his breathing

slow and stertorous. His conscious self seemed absorbed
with the necessity of maintaining those deep, long, sonor-
ous respirations.

The comforting words seemed sucked up into the
vacuum above Don's head, but as Michael Davidson
mouthed the conventional phrases of the mysterious ways
in which God worked, the apathetic lids snapped open, the
unseeing eyes focused, the weary head lifted and the jack-
knifed body unfolded. Stooping over from his full height to
look the astounded chaplain in the eye, Don spoke, slowly
and deliberately, each word falling like acid into a beaker,
from which the smoke of the reaction rose to contaminate
the air.

"You know, Chaplain, do you, that they tell me she was
murdered? Someone poisoned her," he emphasized. "Can
you possibly believe that a madman's destruction of the
sweetest woman who ever drew breath is a manifestation of
God's great design?"

The chaplain faltered to a stop. A pungent silence
enveloped the room's occupants. Murder did not happen
on a university campus! Policemen were called only to stop
the louder drinking parties, not to investigate violent crime.
This was outside the ken of the chaplain's experience. How
had Margaret known he should not go?

He wondered if God had given women such a strong
sense of intuition to compensate them for their lesser
intelligence. The standard words of comfort and help in
bereavement and loss seemed inappropriate now. He had
no customary ritual to rely upon.

His God, however, had endowed him with humanity. He
felt for Don, devastated not only by the loss of his wife, but
by the fact that it had been deliberately induced. And so he
overcame his own feelings of inadequacy and stumbled on,
his voice shaking.

In that way, the chaplain became a source of comfort to
the Benedicts. His obvious sincerity, his horror and genuine
distress provided the impetus Don needed to rouse himself

from the torpor and bewilderment that had engulfed him since Saturday afternoon.

Don sat down again, a little straighter, this time to talk. And, in talking to the chaplain, he began to come to grips with the stark, irrevocable shock of his loss.

"A police official was here today. I forget his name, but that's not important. He was called in by the coroner yesterday. They found an injection mark on her arm when they did the autopsy. They think that she was poisoned. They won't even let us bury her until they know for certain."

Michael Davidson had a sudden unvoiced thought. One did not need a body to have a memorial service. Diffidently he suggested that perhaps Don would feel better if they planned one. So much simpler, less ritualistic. Held in "The Hall" he thought, or perhaps they would prefer it to take place in the smaller university chapel? Then they could have a funeral service later with just the close friends and relatives.

"Perhaps that would be better," said Don. "But I want to wait a few days. I can't face it yet. It's so hard to believe! Saturday morning she was her usual happy self. We'd been out the night before to the alumni dinner. She talked to so many friends. She was radiant, so full of life!"

He stayed pensive and still for a moment before continuing.

"She was still in bed, of course, when I took her coffee in to her the next morning. I had to be at convocation quite early because I was the marshal lining up the students. It would have been very hard for me to spend any time with her at the ceremonies. But she didn't mind that! She was so pleased to be accompanying her old friend from her New York days to convocation!

"When I told her how hard it would be to meet her she asked me if there was any chance she could use the reserved seat that I had been given so she could take some photographs for Alice. Of course I said 'Yes.' I didn't mind standing at the back. I put down her tray, kissed her and that's the last time I saw her."

He paused and blinked. "You see how thoughtful she was of others! She knew Alice would be sitting farther back with the rest of the parents. That thoughtfulness was typical of her. She was always so interested in other people. I can't believe she's dead!" He shook his head, his eyes squeezed tight to block the blighted tears. "She was so vital. What am I going to do without her?"

It was a question without an answer.

CHAPTER NINE

With the tea tray cleared away, and the study tidied, Grace Forrester settled down to some long-overdue correspondence. The Federation of Women Scientists, she read again, felt it imperative she reconsider her decision not to chair a plenary session at their annual conference in Budapest in August. She sat for a long while, chin propped in her thin, veined hand, rereading the most recent exchange of letters. She was framing in her own mind how best to tell an elderly colleague that in her opinion it was time for them both to step aside.

The impetus for this decision was the famous neurologist, whose textbooks were still in force, who had spoken at convocation again after an interval of fifteen years, and who, at his second appearance, had tottered on stage, grasping the lectern with bony hands to keep from falling. He had then proceeded to mouth a speech notable only for its betrayal of the ravages of senility. How sad it was to be remembered for one's frailities, and how much better to retire still admired. The question was how best to tell her scientist friend that their time was past? She pulled the thin, blue airmail sheet towards her and had just begun to write when the doorbell rang.

Grace's credo had always been self-sufficiency. Her sense of self-worth required that she be independent. She had been heard to say that when she was no longer able to be self-sufficient she would appreciate it if someone would have her admitted to Green Park Lodge. The fatal flaw in her perception had always been, however, the fact that her independence had its wellsprings in the security of a home base. To maintain her house required help, for her many commitments took her away from home at irregular intervals. So, for thirty years her help had been Sarah, a plain knob of a female, dour, recalcitrant, and totally devoted to her "Doctor." Total devotion did not extend, however, to keeping her opinions to herself. What Grace felt was self-reliance, Sarah perceived as sheer, unadulterated stubbornness.

"What, for heaven's sake, is the point of hiring a cow and not using the milk?" Sarah would demand in exasperation of Grace's back, bent over mitering the corner of a bedsheet. "Can't you ever learn what's your work and what's mine?" Grace would straighten up, give the spread one last twitch, and explain that no one human should exist to serve another. It was far different, she would explain, for Sarah to manage dinner parties, or oversee the running of the household, than to become Grace's personal slave.

"Slaves ain't paid," Sarah would mutter, smoothing an imaginery wrinkle from the old quilt that served as Grace's bedspread, as Grace left the room. They had not solved the problem of Sarah's job description in thirty years, but had come to a grudging compromise, wherein Grace was allowed to do what appertained to personal care, and Sarah ran the house.

Thus it was, early on that Monday evening, that Grace rose from her chair, put down her pen and answered her own front door, while Sarah, two steps behind, stood in the hall, wiping her floury hands on her apron and rolling her eyes heavenward.

The visitor standing so insouciantly on her doorstep was one of the last persons Grace would have expected to see there, but she was unaccountably pleased. Cold, hard reason might remind her that it was unlike Jamie Dewar to pay his respects to his former teachers, but the personal naïveté that was one of Grace's most lovable characteristics made her beam and hold wide the door when Jamie announced that was why he had come to her home.

He looked curiously boyish as he confessed that not only was he there for old times' sake, but that he was escaping from his relatives and neighbors, whose numbers, it seemed, increased in a logarithmic progression.

"I seem to have acquired a whole new family tree," he remarked, "and they seem bent on introducing me to each little twig." He followed Grace into the breakfast room, and lounged there at his ease, legs crossed at the ankles, one arm in his blue blazer stretched negligently across the back of the chair. Sarah went off to bring them coffee.

He eyed Grace covertly, and made small talk while waiting for the servant to return with their coffee. "Thanks, I take it black," he said, smiling at Grace and effectively ignoring Sarah, hovering with cream jug and sugar pot. He was there for information, but how best to open the conversation? His free hand came up to tug at the knot of his Lockland tie. Then he noticed Grace, seated correctly in her wing chair, try to lift her left arm in its cast unobtrusively onto the chair arm for support.

"Dr. Forrester, you've hurt your arm! I'm so sorry! What happened to you?"

Grace pursed her lips. She did not care to be reminded of something which she regarded as an unfortunate inconvenience.

"Just a stupid slip in front of a hotel in Venice last month, Jamie. It's really of no consequence, so we won't waste time talking about it. Instead, tell me about yourself." She smiled at him. "Since I had the pleasure of being at convocation of course, I know what the president said about your scientific achievements these past few years, but these official speeches never tell us anything about the personal side of life. What's it like to be in the world of international business, for example? Do you ever miss the academic life? Or supervising your own research in your own laboratory?"

Jamie tried to appear suitably modest. "There's no doubt

it's a very different way of life. Much faster pace, weightier decisions. But you know, Dr. Forrester, that it's almost impossible to do meaningful research in a small, academic laboratory these days. The only way to accomplish something nowadays is in industrial research. You need the manpower to carry out your ideas. Why, it took me years to perfect 'Donerin'! Developing and marketing new drugs is feasible only in a large corporation such as I run." He looked persuasively at her and said solemnly, "Banting and Best sound very romantic but the discovery of insulin nowadays would be done much more efficiently by a large corporation. I realized early on I had no choice but to contribute my talents on a larger platform. It unfortunately requires a great deal of travel. I tend to be out of the country half the year, at least. In fact, would you believe my head office is in Switzerland?" He gave a self-deprecating smile.

Grace smiled back but remained silent. His right hand stole to his little finger and he began to twist his signet ring round and round.

"And of course, since I'm no longer married, I don't have the commitments that would require me to stay in one place too long. I'm afraid that Ruth, my ex-wife, just couldn't cope with the responsibilities that go along with being married to the head of research in a large company such as ours. She stayed in Connecticut with our son. I felt terribly sorry for Alexander's sake that she made that decision, but she wasn't happy in the limelight, I'm afraid."

Now Grace did speak. "It must be a pretty lonely life, then, Jamie," she said softly.

He shrugged. "Well, I do have servants," he replied. "If you're really very busy, as I am, and when you have as many responsibilities as I have, you don't have time to consider yourself."

"Does it feel strange to be back at Lockland, Jamie?" asked Grace.

"Very different from being an undergraduate." He laughed. He wished she would not call him by that ridiculous nickname. It conjured up all he wished to forget. His undergraduate existence . . . the loneliness of that first year when he had boarded with a lady from the same sour, fundamentalist sect as his father. Every move spied on and reported back, but not one kindness, not one glass of milk or a cookie after an evening of study.

"Jamie was seen with some girl again last week, Mr. Dewar. A godless hussy," and he'd have to account for his actions when he went home on the weekend.

That had soon ended, though. All it took was that scholarship after first year. It wasn't too hard to beat out your competitors for the prize, not if you knew how to treat the lab assistant in Biology One. A rather plain girl, foolish, but a help. He idly wondered how she'd gotten hold of the examination papers.

She had become quite nasty when she'd found out that he had another girlfriend, but what could she do, without implicating herself? Vindictively, she had told his landlady that he was fooling around with her female roomer, but Jamie was planning on ending that anyway. He wasn't going to ruin his life at that stage by marrying a naïve creature who didn't even know enough not to get pregnant!

Trust the landlady! She'd carried on as if it were her daughter that was pregnant. And she'd kicked her out on the street as she would her own daughter, if she'd had one. He hadn't been around for that mess, fortunately. He was already working. That summer job out in the bush at good pay ensured that he would be able to shake the dust of the Dewars off his heels forever.

Or, at least, until this week, when he had come back on his own terms. Too bad the old man was dead. The elaborate preparations the Dewars had gone to made up for a great deal, but they could never make up for it all.

But he had come here for information. He thought Dr. Grace would still be a cog in the machinations of Marlburg. It was important to him to find out what was going on. He sipped his coffee.

"They tell me some poor old soul died during convocation. I suppose she must have had a bad heart, perhaps been ill for some time? I would hate to think it was the effects of my speech!"

She pursed her lips. At times Grace was oddly old-fashioned. She did not care for levity on such a topic.

"Actually, it wasn't a heart attack and she wasn't that old, at least not from my perspective," she noted gravely. "She'd only been in Marlburg the past three years, just since she married our Dean of Graduate Studies. I'm afraid it's not considered a natural death. The police think she was poisoned." Grace shook her head sadly.

"Poisoned!" repeated Jamie Dewar. "The Dean of Graduate Studies' wife! Why, I knew her! That was Audrey Benedict!"

"You knew her?" Grace looked vaguely surprised.

"Only slightly," he hastily replied. "She was a student when I was at Columbia. Imagine my surprise when she remembered me! She came up to me at the alumni dinner Friday night and introduced herself. We had one of those inconsequential little chats." He wrinkled his nose disarmingly. "In fact, I came across her again the next morning when I was out getting a breath of fresh air before convocation. I didn't know her well, but she seemed pleasant enough, certainly not the type to inspire murder. Hard to believe someone would poison her!"

There, that should do it! Dr. Grace was murmuring something about it being a real shock to the community.

"I would think so! But how was it done? What did they use? Did she drink it before the ceremony, and it took some time to act? Have they found the murderer? I suppose it was her husband? It usually is."

Grace tried to stem the flood of questions.

"As a matter of fact, the police seem to think it was injected, rather than ingested. They're investigating, of course, but they haven't said what the drug was. Nobody's been arrested, but I'm sure it wasn't her husband! Poor Don! He adored her! He's beside himself with grief!"

"I can imagine," said Jamie solemnly. "How awful the whole thing sounds. Poor little Audrey! She was such a sweet, innocent little thing when I knew her, and to think she's come to this." Jamie Dewar looked suitably shocked.

He felt it was clever of him to have looked up Dr. Grace. She had been quite bright in her time. Probably a little garrulous now; the old generally were. So, if she repeated their conversation, so much the better. If only Audrey hadn't had a chance to talk, everything would be all right. He'd explained that meeting in the maze quite well, if anyone had happened to see them. He must remember to ask how Dr. Grace was doing. Retired people generally liked to be considered worthy of consultation. He had early on in his career learned that ploy. Of course, one had to be careful to put a limit on the time one must spend with them.

"Well," he said, "do let's leave sordid topics behind. They certainly don't grace this lovely room. It's delightful to see you looking so well! I'm sure you're keeping busy in your retirement. Have you managed to keep up with any scientific meetings?"

But before she could do more than mention that she had been to a conference in Venice in April, Jamie rose to his feet, put down his half-drunk coffee, and apologized, saying that his many commitments this week made it impossible for him to stay longer, as delightful as it had been.

Grace ushered him out personally, and reflected, as she shut the door behind him, that leopards never change their spots, they merely refine them. She wondered idly what Margaret would make of that aphorism.

CHAPTER TEN

Probably one of the last things Margaret needed at that point was a philosophical discussion of leopards, metaphorical or real. There she sat, involved in a heated exchange with the chaplain. They had finished supper, and were arguing above the dessert plates and coffee cups. This in itself was not unusual. An observer could only comment on the uniqueness of the occasion by noting the site. Usually, their rather vehement discussions occurred in the living room, to which they would repair in deference to their dinner companions.

It is a sad commentary on the ingenuousness of mankind that they expect of their clergy the attributes of their God; and perhaps a sadder one that some of the clergy are unwilling to show that they possess, instead, the attributes of the humans they serve. This criticism could never be levelled at Michael Davidson, however. His passions often ran close to the surface. It was indeed one of the reasons he had been a success in his rather anomalous position. However, he also possessed, as a remnant of his Victorian upbringing, the grace to hide some of his stronger emotions from public scrutiny, when possible.

Tonight, however, the move to the living room had proved unnecessary as there had been only the two of them for supper. The three undergraduates who normally boarded at Margaret's had dispersed for the summer, while Gillian, the free-wheeling spirit who had inhabited the front upstairs bedroom for four years, had graduated on Saturday and joined the enclave of students occupying "The Spit." "The Spit" was a point of beach not far distant from Marlburg and served yearly as a post-convocation celebration site. Gillian had provided ammunition for the Reverend Davidson's weekly sermons for four years, thereby helping, her iniquities being so close at hand, to keep the chaplain in touch with the youth of the day.

Margaret was glad that there were only the two of them that night. She was emotionally exhausted after her afternoon at the Clays', and the supper she had just eaten was the second one she had helped prepare that day. It was wearing to watch interactions of a family such as the Clays' in times of stress.

It was a family that did not pull together, but whose efforts were either feeble and uncoordinated, or disparate, so that an adversary could often pull them over the line in a mental tug of war. She thought how Helen's desperate passions, so out of control, coupled with Ted's gelatinous ineffectiveness and Paul's sullen indifference, produced at best a tangled web, with the two little girls struggling like tiny flies to escape the sticky filaments. She had not liked looking below the surface of the Clay marriage. She thought back forty years to her dead fiancé, and wondered if Ted and Helen had started out with the same high hopes.

She looked around the familiar dining room, the bay window sunny with her plants, the dark varnished faces of her forebears looking down on her, the ornate vases decorated with stylized roses on the mantelpiece, and was glad to be home again, even home arguing with the chaplain.

Now, Christian tolerance and forbearance had no role in the verbal encounters between the Reverend James Michael Davidson and Margaret Matthews McDuff. Their

discussions, usually freewheeling and unmarked by objectivity, served as the outlet for those deep emotions otherwise repressed by their Victorian upbringing. Tonight the topic was police harassment, as perceived by the chaplain. He had already confided to Margaret his horror at the actuality of murder on campus, discussed the idea of a memorial service, and was now launched on a wider sea.
wider sea.

"Margaret, my dear, it is simply the method with which one conducts a police investigation. The first consideration, and I use the word advisedly, must be the bereaved. Now no one could possible argue that the criminal must be brought to justice, and speedily. But in a civilized society it must be done in a way that avoids causing more grief to those who are bereaved. No! Don't interrupt! Today I saw the most subtle kind of police brutality, right here in Marlburg. Can you imagine the callousness of interviewing the bereaved right in the home he shared with his wife, shocking him with a detailed description of the manner of her dying, refusing, actually refusing, to let her be buried, and then — Can you believe it? — asking him to account for his movements on Saturday? I was horrified when he told me that. I think something must be done!"

Margaret settled down to be quietly reasonable.

"As you very well know, they're just trying to do their job," she said sweetly. "Think how much worse it would have been if they had taken Don down to the police station to question him there. Everybody would be sure he was a suspect, then. And he's certainly entitled to the truth, even if it's unpleasant. Heck, murder is unpleasant. Losing one's spouse is unpleasant. Surely everything else becomes inconsequential compared to that. Besides, they have to consider the possibility that he did do it. They probably don't even know him. Statistically it's usually someone very close to the victim."

"Margaret McDuff, I'm ashamed of you! How could you

possibly even think that Don would do such a thing!" The chaplain's beard quivered with emotion.

"I don't think that!" she fired back between clenched teeth, "and I didn't say that! You're not listening! I wouldn't dream of suspecting Don! I can't imagine a more gentle man! But truthfully, speaking in the abstract" — at which point her voice rose perceptibly higher — "and I know I'm an old maid who's never been married, I expect that no outsider ever sees anything in a marriage but what the couple is willing to show. Certainly not until it starts cracking up."

And she thought again of the cracks, widening into gulfs, that she had watched appearing earlier that afternoon.

Just then the telephone rang. Margaret got up slowly to answer it. She was desperately tired. Putting her coffee cup down on the hall table, she stood there, listening quietly in the semi-dark, and occasionally nodding her head, as if her caller could see as well as hear her.

"Yes, of course I will, Grace. Just as soon as I've tidied the kitchen. Yes, in around half an hour. No, I don't mind. The walk will clear my head." She hung up and came back to the table, where the chaplain was regarding her with some concern.

"As you going out again tonight?" he asked.

"Yes, Grace has something she wants to talk to me about," said Margaret, looking curiously at the chaplain. It was unlike him to be interested in her comings and goings.

"Do you think you should be out walking?" he inquired. "There's a murderer loose out there, you know."

Margaret was touched by his concern. "Somehow I don't think he's lurking in the bushes waiting for me to leave," she said, "but if it would make you happier, I'll take a taxi."

"You should," he said. "Until she's caught, you shouldn't be alone anywhere."

Margaret stopped piling the plates.

"She?" she repeated. "Why she?"

"Because it has to be a woman," he replied. "Men don't use poison."

"Oh," said Margaret deliberately, resting both hands on the table, her eyes narrowing. "Why not?"

Even as she spoke, she knew this was the warning bell, the preface to another round, at a time when she was supposed to be on her way, but the remark was one that she could not, in all conscience, ignore.

"Well," he replied, "any student of the *modus operandi* knows that men don't use poison. Women do. They like to be miles away when their victims die. Women don't like to see the consequences of their actions."

"And men do?" responded Margaret sweetly. "Men like to watch their victims die, do they? You paint a fascinating picture of the male mind! How fortunate for the police that they can immediately eliminate half the human race from consideration in Audrey's death!" She went on politely. "Now I can see why, speaking of police harassment, you feel they shouldn't question Don. When it comes time to interview the potential murderesses, is it right for males to be interviewing female suspects, do you suppose? Have you considered demanding female interrogators for female suspects?"

The chaplain looked at her mildly.

"Now that is a good idea," he said seriously, "so long as they report to a male superior officer. Having to arrest someone is a very dangerous business, I expect. I wonder if we should suggest it to them?"

Margaret took the little brush and salver from the sideboard and began furiously to decrumb the cloth, as the chaplain carried the dishes out to the kitchen.

"I should have known better," she muttered to herself, "after thirty years I should have known better. . . ."

She was still muttering under her breath when the taxi deposited her safely at Grace's front door. But when the two old friends had settled down comfortably in front of the fire in Grace's study, Grace's dilemma took precedence.

"I had a visit from Jamie Dewar this afternoon, and while we were chatting he mentioned that he had known Audrey Benedict. Now, I know that it's probably nothing, but I wonder if the police should be told."

"What did he actually say?" asked Margaret.

"Well, I don't think I can recall it exactly. We were talking on a variety of subjects. But he said that the murder — no, he said 'death' — must have dampened the weekend celebrations. When I told him who had died, and I don't think he knew beforehand, he was very shocked. He said that he'd known Audrey in New York when he was a graduate student. Then he said she'd come up to him at the alumni dinner on Friday night, and that he'd run into her again when he was out walking on Saturday morning before convocation. I'm torn between feeling that the police should know all about Audrey's last few hours and feeling that we had a private conversation and that for me to go to the police would be a gross invasion of Jamie's privacy. I'd feel like I was tattling," she ended in explanation.

"Don't you think that's a mite emotional?" asked Margaret. "It wasn't exactly a privileged conversation. I doubt your reputation as a non-gossip is the issue here. If a woman has been murdered your responsibility is to tell the police anything that might conceivably be helpful. I'm sure Dr. Dewar would be the first to agree. You're not accusing him, after all. People are still entitled to meet other people in this world."

"You're right, Margaret, of course. I wonder if I should phone Jamie first? No, that might just upset the family reunion. Did I tell you Dewars from all the nearby counties are gathered together to do him honor? What a justification for Jamie!"

"And what a peculiar word to use! What justification is necessary?"

"Oh dear," said Grace ruefully. "My tongue is loose

tonight." She grimaced. "It's just that when Jamie first came to university, his father insisted that he room with old Mrs. Helland, over on Elm. Do you remember the rooming house she had?"

Margaret nodded. She had had a few rejects from there that she had taken in, plus a few voluntary transfers.

"He had a terrible time. He took Chemistry from me that year, and I remember how repressed and held down he was. A very quick mind, mind you, but you could tell his father held him by some very tight purse strings. A very old-fashioned man! I met the father when he came to see if I was a suitable person to be teaching his son. Anyway, everyone knew that Jamie was having a miserable year, excluding academics, of course, for he had to go and work on the farm on weekends, and with Mrs. Helland, you certainly couldn't have a pleasant social life. I think she was a spy as well as a landlady, you know."

Margaret agreed grimly. "I don't think there's any doubt about that. A hideous woman! She was a self-appointed guardian of other people's morals."

"Anyway, what I'm trying to get at is that at the end of first year, Jamie won a very prestigious award over some very capable people, left Mrs. Helland's and never darkened the farm again. Now the reason I remember this so well, is that there were some questions raised at the time. Something about one of his final examinations. Not in Chemistry, of course, in something else. I think he was accused of having prior knowledge of the examination questions. I don't remember the details, except that it was a bit messy and took away some of the glory of the award. Of course, he's proven himself since, over and over. Look at the wonder drug he discovered, and the position in his company! I was really quite pleased that Andrew heard him speak. But you know, Margaret, many of these great men pay a heavy price personally. Jamie was telling me his marriage has ended, and when he was speaking to me, I couldn't help feeling that he was a very self-centered man. That doesn't make him a murderer, of course."

"Well, he certainly was self-centered when he left Alice Blackstrom pregnant to face the music all by herself!" commented Margaret grimly. "I wonder if he recognized her at the alumni dinner on Friday night? She wasn't looking forward to seeing him again."

"Oh! Why was she there?" asked Grace, momentarily distracted.

"All the trustees have to go," explained Margaret. "She had to leave my place early to go back and get changed for dinner."

"Jamie Dewar certainly never commented on seeing her there to me," said Grace.

Margaret got up to phone for a taxi home. But on the way she stopped and said, "Grace, if I were you, I'd let the police sort it all out. That's what they're paid for, and they're the ones that know what they're doing." She bristled. "And speaking of what they're doing, let me tell you what the chaplain has decided in his infinite wisdom! He's decided the police are harassing Don Benedict. Poor Don! Of course they had to question him. And I thought it was very considerate of them to talk to him at home. But there's no convincing Michael Davidson of that. Also, he's decided the murderer is female, and" — Margaret warmed to her tale — "he's decided, after due reflection, that women, being delicate creatures, must murder indirectly so they don't have to see what they've accomplished. I love the man's mind! After thirty years he continues to astonish me."

CHAPTER ELEVEN

He sat on the very edge of the yellow velvet chair with the curved, spindly legs, his mere size inviting disaster. Grace became distracted by the ominous creaking as he tilted forward to hear more clearly what she was saying. His bulk overwhelmed the delicate chair, the thin bone-china teacup and saucer were lost in his oversized hand, and he loomed far too large in her little study.

She wondered if she should suggest moving to the breakfast room, with its old-fashioned wicker chairs, better designed for his size. But the chair held the while she explained, with unwonted hesitation, her reason for summoning the police to her home.

She had initially intended to telephone, but there had seemed no practical way of handing over the information she wished to impart. She had unfortunately been able to envisage the scenarios.

"Hello, I'm calling to report a conversation I had yesterday . . ." Would she have gotten any further before an audible sigh from the person on the other end, convinced she was a nut case, would have silenced her?

Perhaps she could have started with: "Good morning, I'm calling with regard to the late Mrs. Benedict's last few hours." She could see herself finishing off that story in the presence of her lawyer.

Grace did not need a second opinion to decide that if she

were to be believed it would be better to have her conversation face to face with an official somebody. So it was even better to find that the detective sent to talk to her was someone she knew.

The large, sandy-haired behemoth had been a former student of hers, who had completed his degree at Lockland. Not that he had ever used it in a formal sense. A genetic magnet had drawn him inexorably towards police work. His father, two uncles, and a cousin were all members of police forces, and ever since he had been old enough to voice an opinion it had been Bill Barnes' stated intention to follow family tradition.

He listened quietly and spoke only as Grace came haltingly to the conclusion of her report on her conversation with Jamie Dewar.

"How very nice of you to tell us, Dr. Grace. We had no idea where Mrs. Benedict was between her breakfast in bed and her walk up the aisle at convocation. We'll ask Dr. Dewar very discreetly about seeing Mrs. Benedict Saturday morning. We know that it wasn't he who killed her because he was in public view the whole time before convocation. We suspect she was poisoned shortly before she walked up the aisle."

Grace murmured an involuntary "Oh dear!"

"We'll just have to explain to him why we need a broad perspective. She might have told him something that will help us find out what happened to her. I'm sure such an intelligent a man as he is will understand why we have to talk to him. Don't worry! We can do it very easily without upsetting him. We do this sort of thing all the time. You don't have to tell me that we mustn't offend the Honorary Graduand! Otherwise there might be a little trouble conferring honorary degrees in the future."

And he looked at her comically and spread his huge ham hands, palms up, teacup and saucer precariously balanced, to emphasize his point.

Grace laughed delightedly. Such a big, hulking lug to be

so reassuring! She felt immeasurably better for having told him.

"Tell me what you thought of Dr. Dewar's speech, Dr. Forrester. You did go to convocation, didn't you?"

"Yes, I did, Bill," she replied. "It was an excellent speech." She went on enthusiastically. "Just the sort of speech you want your graduates to hear. Very lucid, stressing what they could expect to achieve if they were willing to work. Parts were inspirational, I'd say, and of course, he himself is an example of how far one can go."

"Well, I'm almost sorry I missed it," he commented. "Convocations aren't really in my line. Barely survived my own, but in the light of what's happened how I wish I had gone to this one! Life might be a little less complicated right now if I had. Tell me, did you see Mrs. Benedict at all at the ceremony?"

"As a matter of fact I did. My nephew and I had seats just five rows back of her. She must have taken over her husband's seat, because she was sitting in the rows reserved for staff. I saw her come in late, after the procession was in. She had an aisle seat, and slipped in very quietly, didn't have to bother anybody. Then, when everything was over, she didn't get up. I guess that was when her neighbors first realized something was wrong. We saw them trying to revive her, and I sent Andrew out to call the ambulance."

"Did you know then she was dead?" asked Bill, putting his teacup down on the rug, next to his feet, and taking out a small notebook and pencil.

"No, not immediately, Bill. I only realized it when I saw how difficult it was to resuscitate her. I thought at first she had fainted. You know how hot it gets in there when there's a crowd! But once they laid her in the aisle and tried — Is the correct term CPR? — then I knew it had to be something quite serious."

She changed tack. "Did you know that one of Andrew's friends had noticed her just prior to her sitting down, while she was still in the lobby? I think he thought she was waiting for someone."

"No, we didn't know that either," he replied. "Dr. Benedict told us that she was planning to go to convocation with a friend from New York, but we haven't found out who the friend is yet. That's probably whom she was waiting for. Her husband had given her his reserved seat so she could get better pictures of her friend's son being hooded. Did you by any chance notice her taking pictures during the ceremony?"

"Now, I don't remember her standing up during the service at all," said Grace, thinking back, "and she would have had to to get a clear view for taking a picture. Most of the parents taking pictures were in the aisles. I think I would have noticed if she had stood up, because she was in front of me and only five rows away, but, of course, I wouldn't like to swear to it. She did have on a very striking yellow outfit, so she wasn't easy to miss."

Bill jotted down a note to check on Audrey's camera. It had not been listed with the effects taken in the ambulance or to the morgue. Someone would have to check with her husband to find out its make, and if, in fact, it was missing. Too late now to search the gymnasium, he thought, but he could have another talk with the janitors. They had been, in Bill's opinion, unnaturally prompt in their refuse collection. Bags and bags of garbage had already gone to the incinerator. He wrote "Lost and Found?" to himself, noting mentally that it could be terribly important to find the camera and develop the film. There might be some pictures taken before the ceremony that showed her unknown friend.

"Who did you say saw her waiting in the lobby?" he inquired.

"A boy called Bob Saunders," she said. "He's a friend of my nephew, well, grand-nephew, to be precise. He left the band to have a cigarette in the lobby just before the processional. I think I said she waited in the lobby for some time, as if she was hoping to meet someone. But then she came in alone."

"Well, we'd better have a talk with him as well. You'd be

surprised at what people remember seeing, things that seemed insignificant to them at the time. Dr. Forrester, may I impose on your patience a little longer? I wonder if you noticed anything in the vicinity of Mrs. Benedict's seat during the ceremony? Anything out of place? Anyone coming up to her during the service? Or did she do anything unusual? Get up, or cry out, or make a small disturbance, have a seizure? I don't know — anything at all?"

He remembered Dr. Forrester's acuteness from his student days, her scientific detachment, her precision, her eye for small detail. He wondered if that acuteness was still there.

Grace hesitated for a moment. She tried to visualize the scene in her mind's eye: There had been parents with cameras crouching at the aisle sides, but no, no one had got as close to the stage as the fifth row. Had anyone come up as far as that yellow dress? No, for her own view had remained unobstructed. She continued her mental assessment. Would she have noticed if Audrey had fainted? Obviously not, since she had not noticed Audrey slumped over until people had tried to move past her. Would she have noticed a seizure?

"Bill," she said finally, as he waited patiently, watching her mental gymnastics with a half smile, "I don't think anyone went as far up the aisle as she was. I might have missed her fainting or trying to leave because I was concentrating on the happenings on stage, but if she had caused any disturbance at all to the people around her, I'm sure I would have noticed, because of course, there would have been their reaction as well. I know nobody tried to help her till the people in the audience were filing out, and that was well after the recessional. I never heard her cry out, or make any sound, either, though sound carries forward, not back to where we were sitting. Why do you want to know about that? Do you think she could have been murdered right in the gymnasium, during the ceremony? In front of that huge crowd?"

"I don't see how she could have been," admitted Bill. "But we haven't found a natural cause of death. Unfortunately, there is a recent injection site on her right arm, at the back. We suspect she was injected with a lethal drug, but we don't know what, or how, or even precisely when. It would certainly be helpful to the Forensic Laboratory if they had some pre-mortem signs to go on."

Not for nothing had Grace Forrester achieved international eminence as a scientist. She filled in what Bill Barnes didn't say.

"You're thinking it's odd she died without terminal death throes, aren't you, Bill?" she said. "She should have made some disturbance before she died! If she didn't, and her death was not due to natural causes, it's because she must have been paralyzed before she died. Most poisons cause terminal convulsions."

Bill Barnes raised his eyebrows and looked quizzically in Grace's direction. Yup, the old girl still had all her marbles. He heaved a sigh of satisfaction and continued his explanation.

"We know, Dr. Forrester, that she had to be alive when convocation began, because she was seen to walk up the aisle under her own power. And we know she was dead when convocation was over. The most logical explanation would be that she had a fatal cardiac arrythmia, but she had too many suspicious signs. The degree of rigor mortis was less than it should have been for the known time of death, and boy, do we know the time of death! She also had this small puncture wound on her right arm I told you about. We know how recent it was because it left a blood stain on her sleeve. We suspect she must have been injected with it during convocation or just before she went up the aisle. Injections generally act within the hour."

"If you're talking about that time frame, Bill," said Grace, her soft brown eyes narrowing in concentration, "it must have been a curare-like drug. Certainly that could cause the delay in rigor mortis; it would have paralyzed her so she couldn't leave, and she wouldn't convulse." She paused for a moment and nibbled thoughtfully on her thumbnail. "But you know what's wrong with that theory? You have to give those drugs intravenously, and they act instantaneously. If it wasn't for that, I would say it would have to be a quaternary ammonium compound."

Bill Barnes looked at his old Chemistry teacher with something approaching awe. She really was a most amazing character! He would have loved to probe her mind further, but there was little else but routine questions that he could think of to ask her.

"Would you remember who sat near her, Dr. Forrester?" he asked, rather mundanely.

"Well, I know that Ted and Helen Clay were sitting beside her. Actually, that's hearsay. I don't remember seeing them myself, but the Clays evidently were the first to notice that she was unresponsive. Now, I couldn't tell you who sat in front or behind her, but those seats were reserved, and there should be a master plan somewhere. That's not to say the people who were sitting there should have been sitting there, of course. Just look at Mrs. Benedict sitting in her husband's place!"

Bill Barnes closed his notebook. He looked up at the elderly lady, sitting primly across from him, sensible, low-heeled shoes planted flatly on the rug, the soft jersey of her dress outlining the spare, bony body. The cuff of her long sleeve was open to accommodate the cast on her wrist. Her soft brown eyes served as windows on an astonishing mind. He smiled in appreciation, stood up, and prepared to go. He held on to her hand admiringly.

"We could certainly do with someone like you on the police force, Dr. Forrester," he said in valediction.

CHAPTER TWELVE

Marlburg is a pretty city of approximately eighty thousand citizens, the more prosperous of whose homes nestle into the hills above the Washigon River. Beyond stretches rocky farmland, where early settlers, first French, then English, scratched out a precarious living. There, later land speculators built miniature communities, seemingly overnight, ostentatiously labeling the newly laid out streets after current heroes: "Rolling Stone Drive," "Bianca Boulevard," etc.

"Marlburg" itself was a contraction of a hero's name, the early settlement having been renamed in honor of John Churchill, Duke of Marlborough, back when it was taken over by United Empire Loyalists. The years since had seen the dilution of the dominant stock with a varied ethnic mix, and the subsequent corruption of the name "Marlborough" to "Marlburg." The city was now primarily a university town, and many of its citizens were employed by Lockland, in one capacity or other.

This circumstance in no way assured Lockland University of the undivided loyalty of its employees. The citizenry of Marlburg was quite capable of making the distinction between Lockland, the source of their paycheck, and Lockland, that suspect environment of radical thought, nestled at the base of ivory towers like an academic Disneyland.

There was, therefore, a well-established gap between town and gown that no one bridged, although the same person could function on both sides of it. This seeming dichotomy could only be accomplished by maintaining a rampant schizophrenia in the population, a feat managed daily in Marlburg.

If one left Old Marlburg and wandered west along the river, past the newest, more exclusive sub-divisions, farther past some yet undeveloped stubbly fields and rocky outcroppings, one came after a while to a point of land composed of fine, white sand. A geologist, of whom there were many at Lockland, could no doubt have explained the origins of this sand dune. For the university graduands who encamped there en masse in an annual spring rite, the origins were of little interest, but the dune itself was essential to the natural order of their lives. It attracted them each spring like lemmings, and in numbers that equalled the black flies.

Shortly after his talk with Dr. Forrester, Bill Barnes began his search for Bob Saunders. He had consulted the student directory, but had some initial difficulty locating Bob by phone. An hour later, Bill was still occupied with ascribing Bedouin-like characteristics to the elusive Bob.

His first success came when he was able to convince Bob's elderly landlady to open her front door to the full length of its chain and talk directly to him. Mustering all the charm that a slightly deaf and totally determined old lady might respond to, especially one who had declared, "Don't know a damn thing," before banging down the phone, and "Oh, you're the Fuzz," on preliminary inspection, he managed to extract from her some vital information. Namely, that although she certainly did not know where he was now or usually, Bob had been observed departing in the company of a sleeping bag, a guitar, some black-fly repellant, and Andrew Forrester.

"You might as well look for the Holy Ghost!" she remarked with finality, firmly closing her front door and sliding home the dead bolt.

It might have been fifteen years since Bill Barnes graduated from Lockland, but he had not forgotten the annual tradition that dictated the campout on "The Spit," nor did he envy the provincial policemen whose responsibility it was, the week after convocation, to turn a blind eye to the minor goings on while controlling the major ones.

It was, therefore, close to noon when Bill took off to stalk his elusive quarry, realizing that he was hampered by the fact that he did not know Bob and that he would first have to find Andrew. Wearing clean beige chinos, sneakers and a gabardine windbreaker, he drove to the Spit and parked his car where the road ended and the dune began. Through the trees ahead, he could see tents pitched like oversized mushrooms under the scrub poplars, small maples and oaks that shielded them.

Alone by one of the barbeques near a two-man tent was a girl in a pink bikini, drying her tousled, wet hair with a large, striped beach towel. She appeared to be the only human awake in the tent community at that hour.

"Excuse me," said Bill Barnes, thoroughly enjoying the sight of her slim, tanned body. "Would you happen to know which tent Andrew Forrester is in?"

She straightened up and eyed him contemplatively. "He's in that large, green, four-man one over there," she replied, pointing back behind her, "two over and one back." She twisted her hair up inside the now wet towel, tucked its end over her head and into the towel edge, bent slightly and disappeared into her tent. Suddenly the black flies had sole possession of the campground.

Bill had no trouble locating the large tent that she had indicated. But a small dilemma now confronted him. It was difficult to knock on a tent. A tentative scratch resulted in continuing silence from inside. He cleared his throat loudly a few times. The silence continued, unabated. So he stuck his head inside the tent flap and called "Hello."

Inside the tent it was gloomy. The dark green walls let in only a diffuse light, by which he could dimly discern four sleeping bags, open and unrolled on the floor of the tent. Each contained a motionless body.

He'd forgotten how soundly teenagers slept, or for how long. A few more "Hellos," in increasing decibels, and one sleeping bag rolled over. Its owner opened reluctant eyes, clapped a hand to his forehead with a stifled groan, lay still for a long, agonizing moment, and then dragged a long, lanky body from its casing like a wet moth from its pupa.

It was a relief for Bill to see that the lanky, red-haired, freckled-face youth, who, sitting up, was staring blearily at him, was Andrew.

"Hi," he said. "Andrew?"

"What's wrong?" replied Andrew, who had by now recognized Bill, and immediately assumed that he was there because of some catastrophe at home.

"Nothing's wrong," said Bill, whispering. "I just want to talk to you. Come on outside where we won't wake the others."

"You couldn't wake the others," said Andrew, speaking in his normal voice. "They're out cold. We didn't get to bed till after four. We had a real good session going last night. We met this fantastic girl from Commerce who can belt it out with the best of them. They're all tired. I'm whacked and I packed it in early. You know how it is!" He shrugged his shoulders expressively.

"Yeah, I vaguely remember," admitted the man whose skill with a clarinet had chilled the night air around the Spit for four college seasons. "I just came to ask you to point out Bob Saunders to me."

"Point out Bob Saunders to you?" repeated Andrew. "Why?" His voice rose in surprise.

"Because I'm investigating Mrs. Benedict's death and he saw her just before she died."

"Oh," replied Andrew helpfully. "That's him there," pointing to a fusiform shape lying on its back with an arm flung dramatically over its eyes. "He's a hard one to wake up. I'd better help you."

He clambered free of his sleeping bag, bent his six foot three over in the murky stillness, and knelt beside the indicated roll. His one hand grasped the exposed shoulder and shook it, meanwhile saying urgently "Bob, Bob!" Receiving no reply, a response he had obviously anticipated, he pulled a recorder from a duffel bag nearby, placed it close to his victim's ear, and unlimbered some rising notes that would have propelled instantaneously many a dead man from his rest. It caused Bob merely to turn sideways into the fetal position, give a piteous moan, followed by a few restrained oaths, and return to slumber.

Andrew, much encouraged by this relative return to consciousness, continued to shake him vigorously by the shoulder now uppermost, and said, "Bob, there's a policeman here to see you!"

This proved to be a mistake. Bob decided this was but misplaced whimsy on Andrew's part. It was not until Bill Barnes' deep baritone also pierced his consciousness that he shook his head resignedly, and got up. The other two occupants of the sleeping bags had reacted to the disturbance much sooner than Bob and were sitting up, each encased from the waist down in quilting, looking enquiringly at the two of them.

"Some things change," thought Bill, noting that the occupant of one sleeping bag was female. "Born too soon," he thought, wistfully.

"Why do you want to see me?" asked Bob, hitting on the nub of the matter. Again Bill went through his explanation. The other two, losing interest, lay down again with a groan. Bob, with a last, longing look at their outstretched forms, resignedly followed Bill through the tent opening into the morning outside.

Blinking and yawning, he seemed dazed by the bright sunshine. Bill led him back to where he had parked his car and poured him out a cup of coffee from the thermos he had had the foresight to bring. It took a while before Bob became technically conscious. It took even longer before he could look at Bill with eyes that were not drooping with sleep.

They leaned against the car, their faces lifted to the warm spring sun, and conversed casually.

"I understand you took some time off from playing during convocation and went out to the lobby for a cigarette?"

"Yes, and it bloody well wasn't worth it! I have had more trouble over that one cigarette!" Bob started to shake his head in disgust, but quickly thought better of it. The night's revels had obviously left him a small legacy. "And it wasn't during convocation," he protested. He held his hands over his temples, his fingers making contact as if he was trying to keep the top of his skull from flying off. "It was actually just before convocation. I was back for the processional march. I was just out there for five minutes, for crying out loud!"

"Hey, hey! Hang loose! I'm not trying to be your watch dog!" protested Bill in turn. "I'm just trying to find out what you saw. I'm told you saw Mrs. Benedict waiting in the lobby?"

"Yeah."

"Was she alone when you saw her?"

"I don't know! She was in a jam of people. I didn't see her talking to anybody, if that helps."

"Of course," said Bill, understandingly. "You couldn't realize she was a marked woman. It's hard to recall things that weren't of interest to you at the time. I appreciate that."

Bob lit a cigarette, stared at it reflectively for a moment and said, "I should definitely give these up!"

"How did you know it was Mrs. Benedict?" Bill went on.

"Aw, she's famous on campus. Besides, I've seen her with her husband sometimes. Once she came to the Music department and kicked up a hell of a stir with Old Liz . . . I mean, Mr. James' about the music we'd played at a concert. Being her, she felt it was inappropiate or not up to standard or something. We never paid much attention to her. She was always mouthing off about something or other. Sure made Mr. James madder than hell that time, though. Never saw him so sore!"

"Can you remember what she was wearing and what she was doing while she was in the lobby?"

"Yep! She was wearing this bright yellow dress. It had short sleeves. You couldn't miss her! She stood out like a search light. She had dark glasses on. The image, you know! Cool. When I saw her she was pressed against the far wall looking towards where the procession was coming from. She was standing on tiptoe. She's not that tall, anyway," he explained. "I guess she was trying to see over all the people still going past her into the gym. I don't know why, but I thought she looked nervous. Didn't go with the cool glasses."

"That's terrific! You've got a good visual memory! Were you close to her at any time?"

"No, I stayed over near the entrance to the gym, so I could get back in a hurry once they got the procession arranged. I only had time for a few drags. I went back inside before she moved away."

"Did you recognize anyone near her? Anyone unusual?"

"Of course I recognized someone near her! There were tons of people I knew. Some of the parents, and some of the faculty, and lots of the students. Even funny old Ray Clark weaved by on his way to catch up with the procession."

"Can you tell me if anybody looked suspicious?"

"Suspicious?" repeated Bob. "You mean like carrying a gun or something? No, they were all hurrying in to get inside before convocation started. Wait a minute, though . . ." He stopped and thought, then shook his head. "No," he said, "that's corny!"

"Tell me what you were going to say," insisted Bill. "Let me judge if it's corny or not. What did you see?"

"Well, there was this woman lurking around outside the lobby doors. She kept peeking her head in and taking a look, then drawing back and disappearing. I never saw her right in the lobby."

"Did you recognize her?" asked Bill.

"Naw, she wasn't anybody I knew," said Bob.

"Describe her to me," said Bill.

"Couldn't have been a parent. She wasn't dressed up," said Bob, thinking back. "She was just wearing ordinary, everyday clothes. She was old."

"How old?" asked Bill.

"Oh, forty, anyway", said Bob. "She wasn't ugly, and she wasn't particularly pretty. Blonde hair, short and waved. She wasn't wearing makeup. Five four or five in height, I guess."

"You're pretty good, fellow!" admired Bill. "Any identifying marks?" He was kidding, but he got a response.

"Yeah," said Bob, consideringly. "She had a red smudge on her cheek."

"Rouge or blood?" said Bill.

"I'd have said paint," said Bob. "It wasn't blood."

"See anyone else interesting?" asked Bill, continuing to mine this promising vein for any remaining ore.

"The only one who interested me was Mr. James. Boy, was I on the lookout for him!"

"And he wasn't there even for a moment?"

"Not even for an instant. You see me still before you, I believe? If he had been there, even for a split second, I would have been pulverized. Dead and in small pieces!" And with that the useful part of the conversation concluded.

CHAPTER THIRTEEN

While Bill Barnes was revisiting the Spit, his superior, Dave Merritt, was at the Clays. He had, of course, called first to set up an appointment, a courtesy which had effectively reduced Helen, busy making order out of chaos, to tears again.

Ted had answered the phone, as he had had to do since Sunday. Although in every other way Helen was back to her usual efficient self, she refused to answer the telephone. It had taken her only a few hours to discover that her unfortunate experience had a silver lining for her friends. How exciting it was for them to be supplied with first-hand descriptions of how it felt to sit next to Audrey's corpse at convocation! They responded with suitable expressions of empathy, and regret, of course, but with a certain air of titillation. Since Helen had found it to be a most unnerving experience, she was ill-prepared to relive it repeatedly for the delectation of her friends. She solved the problem by refusing to talk on the telephone.

What a change! She was used to conducting much of her volunteer work by phone. The extension in the kitchen sat on a little pine desk that she had had built so that she could organize her charitable works from what she referred to as her "nerve center." The little cork bulletin board above the desk was festooned with myriad appointments for the children, cards for meetings of social agencies, as well as the

Clays' social engagements. The duty roster for the Psychiatric Institute Gift Shop for May was there, as well as the new one for June that Helen had completed, duplicated and mailed out to her corps of volunteers.

Ted abhorred the telephone. Uncomfortable talking to people he could not see, he had always left any business affairs for Helen to deal with, unless dire necessity dictated his involvment. Consequently his conversations were abrupt and monosyllabic.

Now he had become his wife's official answering service. He acquired this new job description shortly after the first phone call to Helen the very night of convocation. One of her closer friends had called to confirm whether a rumor she had heard was actually true. Helen had started out well enough, although her hand crept to her throat as she talked. Only when she told of getting up and being unable to brush by the body did she falter. Ted could hear the "You didn't! Oh, how awful! Did you know?" tumbling out of the receiver as Helen dropped the phone from nerveless hands and burst into tears. He had hung the telephone up for her with a curt "She can't talk about it anymore," to the gibbering soprano on the other end. He was now dealing equally abruptly with phone requests for volunteers, the children's car pools, and social obligations.

Helen no longer displayed any interest in the phone, her former lifeline. She paid no attention when it rang, answered listlessly when forced to speak, and dropped it lifelessly if Audrey Benedict was mentioned. Otherwise she seemed all right.

Now Ted came back from making an appointment to meet Dave Merritt to tell Helen that the police would be asking them for an official statement on Audrey's death in about an hour. Helen looked at him, eyes meeting his for the first time in days.

"I can't talk to him, Ted!" she explained desperately. "You know that! I don't want to have to describe it!"

"We don't have a choice," he replied. "He's a policeman.

I couldn't tell him not to come. We're going to have to talk to him sometime. There's no reason not to. After all, we did sit next to her. It'll look peculiar if we refuse to talk to him."

Her lower lip began to tremble, her jaw working, the familiar signals of incipient hysteria strung along the halyard of her nerves like so many warning flags.

"Oh, Helen, please!" he begged. "I told them to come at ten o'clock. If we don't talk then, we'll have to do it some other time. Don't make me talk to them alone. I want us to tell the same story. Why don't we just get it over with?"

An hour later Dave Merritt met the Clays and interviewed the two together as they sat nervously on the couch to the right of the fireplace in their family room. The fireplace was unswept, but otherwise the room was in apple-pie order. Helen had seen to that.

On the hearth stood a large pottery vase, filled with an exquisite array of iris spikes. Beneath the soft blues and purples, around the curved pottery base, brushed a Siamese cat, its kinked tail waving high against the lower florets. On various end tables stood other bowls, one holding a mass of peonies. Another, smaller, of crystal, held white violets and the small bells of lily of the valley. Ted had made his contribution.

They sat close together, but not touching. Helen avoided meeting Dave's eyes, except momentarily when they were introduced. Ted had given him a limp handshake.

A faded, pink ribbon held Helen's blonde hair tied back behind her neck and she was wearing a clean, white blouse and striped denim skirt. She had ironed them within the last hour, although Ted had found that she had uncharacteristically forgotten to unplug the iron. Pink lipstick, newly applied, made a moist slash across a face drained of all natural color.

Ted had just come in from the garden. He was still in his working clothes, an old pair of jeans and a faded, cotton-knit T-shirt. He had, however, washed the dirt off his hands, shaken Dave's hand limply and ushered him into the family room. He switched off the television as he offered Dave a seat.

The smell of fresh coffee came from the kitchen, but neither Helen nor Ted remembered to offer some to Dave. Dave took the proffered seat on the far side of the fireplace facing them. He spoke softly and pleasantly, taking no notes.

"I'm sorry to have to bother you," he said. "How unfortunate that you happened to be the ones sitting next to Mrs. Benedict when she died! I won't take long, I promise, but you could help us with some questions we have to get answered."

"My wife has been very upset by this unfortunate episode," said Ted. "I hope you won't upset her further, because it really was rather dreadful to go through, and it makes it worse every time she has to go through it again."

Immersed as she was in her own misery, Helen seemed unaware of her husband's unaccustomed gallantry. Ted sighed. He, too, was not looking forward to being interviewed.

"I'll try to make it as quick and easy as possible," promised Dave.

"I don't know when she died," said Helen, initiating the discussion, her voice a toneless monotone. "We were already sitting down, waiting for the ceremonies to start. The academic procession came in, and then suddenly she was there sitting beside me, and then, and then . . . she was dead!"

"Can you describe to me exactly where you were sitting, Mrs. Clay, and who was sitting near you?"

"We were sitting right near the stage, in the reserved section, in the second row on the left-hand side. My husband had a reserved seat, because he is Faculty, and I was representing the Faculty Wives' because our president couldn't come and I'm the secretary. I can't remember who sat in front, or behind us. Ted was sitting on my left and she . . . came and sat right beside me."

"I came in before Helen," contributed Ted. "I walked

over, because Helen came early with the car, and I still had some things left to do in the garden. I know George Wright was behind me, because I turned around to talk to him until Helen came. By the time Helen came in, the gym was almost full up, and the ceremony started almost immediately."

"I was there before the procession started," protested Helen. "I had to make sure everything was ready for the reception afterwards," she explained, "so I came early, as Ted said. The Faculty Wives' always organizes the reception. But I was in my seat before the actual ceremony started. The only empty seat when I came in was . . . hers. She came in late. I would never do that."

"So Mrs. Benedict came in after you were seated and the procession had already gone by and was being seated. Had the ceremonies started before she sat down?"

"Well, I'm not really sure when exactly she sat down, because it was an aisle seat, and she didn't have to disturb anybody to get to it." Helen seemed to be gaining composure as she spoke. "I didn't even look at her until it was time to go."

"Would you have noticed if Mrs. Benedict made a sound? Did she speak, or make any funny movements? Did you think she was in trouble at any time?"

"I wouldn't know if she moved at all, because I never looked at her, but I didn't hear her speak. The ceremonies were very impressive, you know, and I was totally absorbed."

"She didn't stand up for the benediction," noted Ted suddenly. His wife turned and looked at him, her face a mask.

"Yes, but I thought that was because she didn't believe in religion or something. I didn't know she was in trouble. You don't expect to be sitting next to somebody while they're dying, you know."

"Well then, when did you first notice that something was wrong?" came the soft question.

Here we go, thought Ted. This is the one that sets her off.

Helen's hands clenched and unclenched. He knuckles whitened. Her rings bit into her palm. Her face stiffened with the tremendous effort she was making not to cry.

"When she wouldn't move when I got up to leave. I had to hurry out to make sure they were putting the food on the tables and she wouldn't let me by."

"This is the part that upsets her so," commented Ted, rather unnecessarily.

"Just a few more questions then, and I'll be done. Do you know if anyone came near her and talked to her during the ceremony, or stood near her to take pictures, or anything relevant at all?"

"I don't think anyone talked to her, and I don't know if anyone came up to take pictures or not." Helen, past the crucial question, had regained some composure. Ted was still nervous. He felt his time to be questioned had not yet come.

"Did either of you see Mrs. Benedict before you entered the gymnasium? Say, in the lobby?"

Both Ted and Helen started to speak at once. "I never noticed her!" said Helen shortly. "I saw her standing there!" answered Ted. "She was there when I came in, and I came in a good five minutes before you appeared."

"Well, I was hurrying and I didn't see her," said Helen, glaring at her husband. "I wanted to be sitting down before the procession came in and I could see them coming along down the corridor."

Dave thought it best to intervene. "Did you stop to talk to her, Dr. Clay?"

"Me, talk to her? Of course not!" said Ted. "She had bigger fish than me to fry, I can assure you!"

"Can either of you think of anybody, or any reason why anyone would want to kill Mrs. Benedict?"

Dave watched them sympathetically. He knew what an ordeal this was for lay people. Our society has sanitized natural death with euphemisms. People do not "die," they "pass on." There are no euphemisms for murder. Murder brings death forcibly in front of our reluctant eyes.

"I can't imagine anyone wanting to kill her. She was really an insignificant woman. I felt sorry for her. . . . She didn't have any children, or do any important work. We really didn't have much in common, so I didn't know her well." Helen was vehement in her denial.

"On the contrary, I think she was probably a very powerful woman behind the scenes," argued Ted Clay obstinately. "I suspect you'll find she had many enemies in the university community. Whether something she did mattered enough to any of them to kill her is another matter."

"Well, someone killed her, so she must have done something," thought Dave Merritt, musing over this bitter last remark as he drove back to the station, his interview concluded.

CHAPTER FOURTEEN

A rather sunburned Andrew had been sitting in the waiting room for some time, holding an unread magazine on his lap. No magazine could rival the adventures displayed before him, for this was the lobby of an emergency room. He was sitting front and center before the stage of life: The drama of the large double doors of the ambulance bay sliding open to admit stretchers bearing blanketed still forms, the anxious companions who sat in front of the receptionist fumbling for insurance numbers in wallets and handbags, the impatient parents waiting for adolescents with minor bruises, a weeping wife led outside by her friend. The major tragedies and minor frustrations of life telescoped in time before his eyes as he waited for Penny to finish work.

It was not a world he would want to be a part of. He recognized in himself an unwillingness to participate in that particular drama, a reluctance to work where there was an impromptu situation waiting for him in the wings, where he would have to cope with whatever disaster was disgorged from beyond those sliding glass doors.

But, sitting here watching mini-dramas in which he could play no part was interesting, and he could appreciate how others would feel a sense of worth playing on that particular stage. He wondered if the doctors he was watching, ceremonially garbed in their white lab coats, stethoscopes dangling carelessly from their necks, saw themselves as players, ranked in   hierarchy. There were the Staffmen, their star billing permanently inscribed on plaques on the wall — "Dr. Angus Smith, Urology"; the residents, engaged for the run of the performance, names chalked on a blackboard; the students, only name badges, bit players, here today, on another service tomorrow. Did they actually believe in the roles they were playing? It was thoughts like those that kept him, a voyeur, from being bored.

But now the waiting room was almost empty. The large clock high on the waiting-room wall seemed to tick off the minutes of intermission more slowly. And then he saw her, walking down the corridor leading to the Emergency Ward, her three-cornered smile appearing as she saw him, and her step a little faster. He rose to meet her.

"Hi," she said, "you look like you've had a fun day!"

"Hi," he replied. "You must have had a long one!"

"Oh, Andy, it's been awful! Nobody's in a good mood. The wards are jammed, and we've had eight deliveries since midnight, and they can barely get one room clean before someone else delivers. There must be a full moon."

He took her hand and squeezed it. "Bad day, too, huh?" he said sympathetically.

"Well, on top of everything else, the police have been here, checking the narcotic sheets, and medication cupboards on the delivery floor, and questioning the supervisors. You've never seen such confusion! Finally, Miss Shouldice told them to take themselves and the hospital administrators away and not come back until we'd had a chance to regroup. Everyone practically cheered!" She smiled wearily, pushing her long, dark hair behind her ear. "I'm so glad you waited!"

"I didn't mind," he said, looking lovingly down at her. "It's been interesting, seeing what goes on around here. But you're so tired! This wouldn't be the life for me! I need my sleep! Not necessarily at night time, mind you," he laughed, thinking of his night on the Spit, "but I require my normal amount of sack time sometime during the twenty-four hours provided."

"It's still worth it to me," she defended herself. "I know I'm tired, working since yesterday morning, and not getting any sleep last night. And today was really a strain, because of the hassle the investigators were causing, but that's unusual. Deep down I really love it."

"Why?" he asked, curiously.

"I think it's because Obstetrics is such a happy field! And there's more to it than just that! There's enough critical judgment needed to make it challenging, and occasionally there are problems, so when you get a solution to them it makes it exciting!" She looked up at him confidingly. "And then you get the rewards! I must have watched thirty deliveries and I still get tears in my eyes each time I watch a baby being born!"

"Do you want to be an obstetrician, Penny?" he asked, walking outside with her, their fingers entwined. The glass door that had opened automatically before them, now shut out the world behind them.

"I sometimes think I do, and other times I realize I haven't seen enough yet," she replied. "I start Psychiatry tomorrow, and perhaps I'll want to do that." She shrugged her shoulders. "I only know right now that I don't want to be a surgeon."

"Really?" he asked, interested. To him surgery had the most glamor: gloved hands poised to make the first incision, the bright lights, gruff commands to go with the urgency of the moment.

"I know I haven't the right personality," she commented. "You have to be aggressive, more convinced of yourself than I am. I think I question everything too much to do surgery successfully. But, Andy, you should see the twins we had today! Tiny premature twins, a boy and a girl. Twenty-nine weekers. Just twelve hundred grams or so each!"

"You know, Penny, all my lab work may be metric, but I

still expect babies to come out in pounds and ounces."
Andrew laughed, enjoying her effervescence.

"Well, they're not quite three pounds each. There were anaesthetists and neonatologists all over the place! Talk about organized chaos! It took quite a while to get the boy breathing on his own. They're both on ventilators, but when I went up to the nursery to check on them before I left, they were already reducing the oxygen. The parents are on Cloud Nine! You see, that's what makes it so worthwhile."

"You think they're going to make it, at that weight?" marveled Andrew. "Three pounds of butter each?" They had left the hospital, and by now were walking towards Penny's apartment, across a field where sandlot baseball games were popping up with the dandelions.

"They're being ventilated, but that's certainly what they told the parents," replied Penny. "Andy, can we skip the movie tonight? I don't think I'm up to waiting in line without dinner."

"Now it's funny you should say that," said Andrew. "My thought exactly! I thought instead we'd go down to Dinty's and have spaghetti, take the long way back through the park, and meander along the riverfront. I promise not to keep you out too late. What time do you have to be up in the morning?"

"Psychiatry rounds are at eight," said Penny. "I shouldn't miss those. But spaghetti at Dinty's sounds super! Does the wallet stretch to spaghetti à la Caruso?"

"Yes, and a carafe of house wine too!" Andrew looked down at the triangular face turned up expectantly towards him. He felt so protective towards Penny. She appeared so tiny and fragile, and yet he knew her appearance bore no relationship to the exigencies of her work. She had spent the night without sleep, and worked all that day, while he had lazed around acquiring a sunburn on the Spit. He knew that she would resent any special favors that implied she couldn't cope. Yet, he felt an overwhelming urge to guard and shield her, especially on nights when she was so obviously tired. He drew her closer to his side as they walked on, his arm protectively around her.

"Off we go, then," he said lightly. "Think you can make it the rest of the way or shall I carry you?"

"Oh, Andy," she laughed, "All six-foot-three of you! Someone would think you were abducting me! Not that they could find a policeman! They must all be at the hospital. They haven't found the missing drug yet, you know, and someone said until they find out where it came from, they won't be able to find out who used it."

CHAPTER FIFTEEN

On Marlburg's north side, near the technical college, the bottling plant and a large trucking depot, stands a long, low, one-storey building. Having been built within the last twenty years, it is considered "modern" by the townspeople, although its design is utilitarian rather than *avant garde*. Its setting, however, overlooking a tributary of the Washigon, is magnificent. The field in which it was originally sited has been transformed into terraces, and softly rolling, green lawns. The harsh, box-like lines of the building are softened by foundation plantings of yew, juniper and cedar, dark backgrounds for scarlet geraniums, newly planted. Here and there, from the vast vistas of lawn the canna lilies rise above the dusty miller, begonias, and geraniums in the ornamental flower beds, like the fountains of Versailles.

Vandals know better than to disrupt these flowerbeds, for the squat building, set like a giant's misplaced domino on a green baize cloth, houses the Marlburg Police Department. The surroundings, seemingly so at variance with the buildings, are a testimonial to the former Chief of Police, whose hobby was horticulture, and who willed money to the city for landscaping to hide the barrack-like contours of the building he had so sincerely loathed.

Six feet inside the double front doors is a long counter, behind which can be found an efficient young policewoman, hours eight to five, extracting sums of money from the public for parking-meter infractions. Behind her is a glassed-in room, with two desks, a video display communications unit, telephones, and two brawny constables. This "communications room" caters to the everyday, civic business of lost dogs, stolen bicycles, "break and enter" and theft.

Skirting the communications room, and perpendicular to the counter that serves as first contact, runs a corridor, with multiple doors leading to the offices running off it. The farther along the corridor, the higher ranking the official secreted behind the door, and consequently the more imposing the crime being investigated. The corridor ends in double doors opening onto a committee room. Rectangular and large, the room is dominated by a long wooden table, around which are placed padded, brown leather arm chairs. Heavy glass ashtrays stud the shiny surface of the table at regular intervals. From the walls stare former police chiefs, each in uniform, each with a bronze plaque noting his name and service dates. The horticulturist is placed third from the left and seems a little less stern than the others.

Students of psychology find it fascinating to note that when this gloomy structure was designed, the criminal element was forgotten, and those felons requiring incarceration prior to sentencing, or the drunkards sleeping it off, have to be transported thirty miles to the county jail in Denham. Unsullied by the deprived or the depraved, the building stands as a monument to administration.

On the Wednesday after convocation, one could find beyond the closed blue door halfway down the corridor (dare one mention that each office achieved individuality by the color of its door?) Dave Merritt and Bill Barnes, the former seated behind his scarred wooden desk, the latter sprawled in a chair, legs outstretched, massive hands clasped behind his head. The desk top was littered with books and papers, among them the autopsy report on Audrey Benedict, newly arrived from the Provincial

Forensic Laboratory in a bright green folder, a reference book on drugs, and a seating plan of convocation.

On the dark green blotter, half hidden by the morass of paper, was a pad of paper Dave used for doodling. President Kennedy-like, for Dave doodling became the physical expression of his thought processes, and from the number of swirls and designs dotting the page, he had been thinking furiously. His ballpoint pen, propelled almost spiritualistically, drew an outsize bumble bee as he spoke.

"Let's play "W's"," he said, assigning antennae to the bee. "Some we got, some we may have, some we don't."

"Put them all together, they spell "Murder", a name that means so much to me!" said Bill, facetiously.

"Audrey Benedict is dead. Not buried but dead. We've got the 'who'."

"Sounds like a rock group to me," interjected Bill, earning himself an expressionless stare from Dave, who went on: "Now you could say 'when' is either Saturday, when we know she died, or Sunday, when the coroner called in the troops."

"That day's delay is costing us dearly," Bill noted grimly, his mood switching. "We're a day late collecting evidence from the gym; we're a day late locating the people who might have been around her; we're a day late for people's recollections."

"However, the good news is we've just had 'what' confirmed," Dave announced. "The pathologists suspected she'd been injected with a poisonous substance, and this —" Dave tapped the bright green folder in front of him — "confirms it."

"O.K., what was it?" asked Bill, abruptly sitting upright, his eyes intent, watching as Dave reopened the folder, and held the paper at arm's length. He refused to give in to bifocals while his arms were long enough, he said.

"Never heard of it before," he commented. "Something called 'succinylcholine chloride,' a 'quaternary ammonium compound.'"

"That's what Dr. Grace suspected!" said Bill excitedly. "Trust the old girl to come through! It's a paralyzer."

"Yeah, I've been looking it up," replied Dave laconically. "Used by anaesthetists to get deeper relaxation during surgery."

"But it's generally used as an intravenous drip, because it takes effect almost instantaneously and doesn't last long, isn't it?" queried Bill. "At least, that's what I read."

"Yeah, I know," replied Dave. "The medics almost gave up there because that injection mark was certainly not over a vein. Not that you could imagine Mrs. Benedict allowing herself to be injected intravenously as a sideline during convocation, anyway. No other needle tracks on her, so she wasn't a junkie, getting the wrong fix. However they've sent us some literature, and just at the end it mentions giving it intramuscularly in children. They figure the killer had a strong solution and stabbed her with it fast!"

"He must have got her in the back of the arm when he was behind her. Probably got up close to her and did it in the lobby when it was crowded. She must have thought she was being jostled by the crowd. We know she stood there for some time."

"Yeah. So by the time she got to her seat it would have started working. It evidently hits the large muscles first, like her arms and legs, so then she couldn't get up and leave; then her face, so she couldn't ask for help even if she wanted to, and finally it attacks the respiratory muscles, so she quit breathing. And you know what's really macabre? She would be conscious throughout. That's a bloody bizarre way to go!"

"Do you think we've nailed it?" asked Bill. "Will it stand up in court?"

"I would think so," replied Dave, "if we can find who had access to it. Dammit, this was no spur-of-the-moment decision. Somebody thought it out very carefully."

"So whoever did it had to know how to get hold of the drug, and what it did."

"Exactly! And that's how we're going to find him!

Furthermore, he must have known it was almost impossible to detect. The Lab says it's a very hard drug to trace, because it's broken down quickly, and its breakdown products are ones normally found in the body. If the Lab hadn't been warned what to look for, they would have missed it. They couldn't get a trace from the puncture site, or her blood. But they did find a large amount in her urine. Here, I'll read it to you. There's some jargon here about gas chromatography. Here's the relevant bit. 'The red-violet band scraped from the cellulose plate, and esterified.' Seems you get three esters from the scraping. That identified it. Now they go on to say that the double check is another test using cholinesterase on half a cellulose plate, and making the substance disappear."

"There isn't a hope in hell we're ever going to find that syringe in the gym now, you know," said Bill. "But we've got to go down and talk to the janitors again and ask if they picked one up. It's too much to expect that someone would remember where it was picked up! I wonder if she could have been injected with it while she was sitting down?"

"Doubt it," shrugged Dave. "No one sitting on her right, where the needle track was. The guy behind her was the Dean of Commerce, and I can't see him getting away with pulling out a syringe during convocation and no one noticing. No, I think the "where" has got to be the crowded lobby. You know," he continued, reflectively, "it doesn't really matter if we find the syringe in the gym or not. It'll have been too well handled by now. But the one thing we do have going for us is the drug itself. It has to be someone who knows how the drug acts and has access to it, so that's where I think we should concentrate the bulk of our investigation."

"I'll tell the guys at the General to check for that specifically, and talk to the personnel in the operating room about it."

"I hope they keep good records. And we also have to talk to purchasing, though I doubt if they know how it works."

"Dr. Grace knew how it worked, and she's a chemist. The

university is probably crawling with chemists. Also they have pharmacologists and they'll be experts too. I wonder how readily available it is?"

"Well, we'll have to find out. Isn't Dr. Dewar a chemist?"

"Yup," replied Bill. "He's head of a research department in a big drug firm too, and he knew Audrey Benedict."

"Whoa, there! Let's not take quantum leaps just yet," warned Dave, putting the folder down. "I don't think the university would care to have its Honorary Graduand suspected of murder, just because someone he hasn't seen in years is killed while he's in town. Besides, it might be a little inconvenient to halt the procession, saunter over to the lady in question, say, "Hi there. Imagine meeting you here!" inject her with this poison, hide the syringe in the sleeve of his gown and go on to give his speech. Besides, why would he want to kill her?"

"If we knew the 'why' we'd have the 'who,'" said Bill stubbornly. "There's got to be a reason. Maybe there's a motive in his past. Stranger things have happened. But I admit, it would be difficult to prove. He'd have had to be a bloody fool to try it."

"O.K., who else can you think of who had a motive?" persisted Dave, turning over the pad and embellishing the old designs.

"From all accounts, it would be simpler to ask who didn't," replied Bill, sardonically. "There are a slew of candidates for that particular honor. From what I can gather, she's managed to antagonize everyone she ever came in contact with, from the chaplain to the Head of the Music department, and I haven't even started asking yet."

"Well, who were her friends, then?" inquired Dave. A stiletto with blood dripping from it appeared beneath his busy pen. "Where's the lady she was taking pictures for?"

"I asked her husband about that," said Bill, "He says he never met the lady personally, but he thinks she was a trustee's wife whom Mrs. Benedict ran into at the alumni dinner. She spent a long time talking to her that night. She told him she was an old friend from her student days in New

York. The lady's name is Alice and she wanted to get some pictures of her son's graduation, but she wasn't used to taking pictures. Her husband couldn't because he was sitting with the trustees, so Audrey offered to sit in Dr. Benedict's seat and take the pictures."

"And where is Alice?" inquired Dave.

"Haven't found her yet," replied Bill. "We checked to see which trustee's wife is named Alice, but we've drawn a blank so far."

"If Mrs. Benedict was supposed to be taking pictures of her friend's son she probably didn't have time before the drug took effect. However, she may have taken some pictures before, maybe of her friend. Better get that film developed. Send someone over to pick up the camera from the morgue, if you haven't done it already."

"Wasn't there."

"You're kidding! Could it have been left in the ambulance or in the gym?"

"You'll never believe this," said Bill, enjoying a small measure of superiority. "Her camera never left home! It's still in their house."

"You mean she forgot to take it?"

"Or else she was lying to her husband. Maybe she planned to use Alice's camera."

"Or else Alice may have come expressly to kill her. Maybe she doesn't even have a son graduating!"

"So why did she tell her husband all about Alice? And why did she need his seat?"

"Maybe she was meeting someone else!"

"Yeah, the murderer!"

Dave twirled around in his swivel chair to face the window. Through its dusty pane he could see a little boy on the banks of the creek below, casting a fishing line. "Crazy business," he said. "Could be out there like that kid, relaxing, enjoying life. Instead here we are, chasing some unknown lunatic with a long needle who likes to jab it into people and kill them."

CHAPTER SIXTEEN

Bill stood patiently next to the long counter with its retorts and burners and sinks, while Ray Clark, his papers hurriedly stuffed into his shabby, worn briefcase, established himself on the high wooden stool he had insisted was the one place where he would be interviewed. He trailed one hand in the nearest sink and played with a funnel he found lying there, while Bill talked.

There were some aspects of a policeman's life more futile than others, Bill decided, and finding Ray Clark to be the only member of the Chemistry department around when he was supposed to check for succinylcholine chloride there ranked high on his futility list.

"I'm a lush, you know," remarked Ray complacently, chin up and weaving slightly on his stool. "Jamie Dewar is a bi-i-g suc . . ." — he hiccupped — "success, and I'm a lush. He's got all the money, and I get to teach in his good old Alma . . . Alma Mater. Isn't that fun? But you know," he went on, smiling inanely, "they'll tell you that money doesn't bring happiness. The hell it doesn't! That kind of money buys a lot of happiness!" He hiccupped again for emphasis.

"You're right, I'm sure," said Bill, agreeably. "But I've come here to find out if you know of anyone here who works with any of the quaternary ammonium compounds in their research, or has some available."

"I don't make drugs any more," said Ray. "I used to make drugs, but that was before I concentrated my energies on being a lush. Now I drink. Would you like a drink?" he asked hospitably, picking up a beaker and reaching behind a jar of distilled water for a bottle. Imperceptibly, Ray was managing to alter the environment so that the atmosphere was more convivial. The stool had become a bar stool, the counter a bar, the beakers glasses. Bill had the uncomfortable sensation that he was conducting an interview of a potential witness in a bar.

"Um, I'm afraid I can't drink on duty, so no thanks," said Bill. Ray had succeeded in undermining his authority in the situation and now he understood why Ray had insisted that the interview take place in the laboratory. The investigation of the Chemistry department, he realized, was really going to be useless unless he could talk to someone else.

"Where is everybody?" he asked, looking around him at the empty laboratory.

"They're off at the departmental picnic," answered Ray. "I don't go to those. They drink too slowly for me. But you asked me something before . . . oh, yes. I remember!" He got down solemnly from his perch and put his hand over his heart. "I never did, never had, and never shall have quaternary or any other ammonium compounds in my possession. They are very, very danger-hic-ous." He clambered unsteadily back on his stool and added a colorless liquid, that Bill thought must be lab alcohol, carefully to the distilled water already in his beaker.

"Well, thank you very much," said Bill, closing his notebook and preparing to leave.

"Now, I could make an exception for that bastard, of course."

"Um, what bastard are you referring to, sir?" asked Bill, turning around.

"The great, magnificent, J. Richardson Don't-er, of course," jeered Ray, replacing his arm in the sink, as tenderly as if it were a newborn baby. "He's a right proper bastard, you know. If he wanted something badly enough, he'd go for it, no matter what. He'd kill, if it was important enough. And if he wasn't going to get caught, of course."

"Really?" said Bill noncommittally. "Why would he want to kill Audrey Benedict?"

"That's what I haven't been able to figure out," said Ray, who suddenly seemed to be cold sober. His eyes looked directly into Bill's, he forgot to sway, his speech was clear. "What would she have that he wanted? She wasn't good looking, she wasn't rich, she wasn't a chemist he could steal ideas from." He tilted forward on the stool, breathing alcoholic fumes into Bill's face, and whispered conspiratorially: "She had power here, but her kind of power wouldn't touch Jamie Dewar now!"

"Perhaps she knew something he didn't want others to know about?" suggested Bill, fascinated in spite of himself by the man who was once again weaving in front of him. It made him feel like a snake charmer wooing a rather benign old snake.

Ray poured out the contents of his beaker. He hesitated, eying the big policeman, choosing his next words.

"Nah, how would she have anything on Jamie?" he asked, consideringly. He seemed to be weighing the options. "He hasn't been back here since he was an undergrad. And she's only been here a few years. Now me, I've got lots, lots and lots, on Jamie Dewar. Did you know he stole my work and made a fortune from it? Can't prove it though. Isn't that sad? That's why I'm a lush," he explained. As if reminded of his responsibility to appear in character he picked up his empty beaker and reached again for his hidden bottle.

"Got to keep the old blood level in the alcohol stream diluted, you know," he said, leering at Bill.

"How come he took your work?" asked Bill suddenly.

"Trusted him," came the short, sharp reply.

"Trusted him?" repeated Bill.

"Yeah, trusted him. We worked together on an idea I had when we were at Columbia as Post Docs. One day he was there, and the next day he had gone to a job somewhere, and all the lab books were gone with him. He said he must have packed them by mistake, and that as soon as he unpacked, he'd return them. Next thing I knew, he had a patent application in for "Donerin," he called it. I was too poor to sue. They didn't really go in for Legal Aid in those days, and because we were doing it on our own time, I hadn't any proof."

"That's terrible!" said Bill. "That's fraud!"

"I didn't want all the glory for myself," said Ray. "I would have been happy to share it. Think what we could have done together! Now look at me!"

"But that doesn't explain how someone got hold of this succinylcholine drug and killed a lady during convocation," said Bill, suddenly remembering the reason for his mission to the Chemistry department.

"I don't know either," said Ray abruptly, terminating the conversation by sliding off his stool, his knees buckling, like a puppet with its strings cut. "We don't have any here and I don't think anybody could make it. But lots of people would know how it worked. You'll have to excuse me," he said conversationally, "my body generally folds before my mind. That's why I'm sitting here. It'll take a little while before my mind gets some peace," he confided. "Sort of the same action as succinylcholine chloride," he observed, sliding farther down on the floor.

Bill decided he would wait for the departmental picnic to be over and interview the Head of Chemistry. Ray watched him leave, eyes half shut, his head propped up against the stool's cross bars. Bill was disarming. Ray had almost said too much. He had almost told Bill that Audrey and Jamie had lived together in New York. He thought it preferable to keep quiet about that relationship. If the police knew about it, it would be a short step for them to discover that he, too, had known her in New York. That bitch! He summoned up tears of self-pity, and then angrily wiped them away.

Audrey had supposedly been a friend of his in New York

when he and Jamie were working together and she was living with Jamie. Fine friend she was! If she had only warned him that Jamie had been offered a job back in Canada and that they were splitting up! Even if she had just told him that Jamie was stealing their work book from the laboratory, he could have stopped Jamie then!

How different his life would have been. He would have made the fortune instead of Jamie! He had some good ideas for improving on their new drug. He would have handled it differently. Not sold out to the first drug firm that came along. They could have won a Nobel Prize for that work! He and Jamie Dewar. He could see himself up at the lectern in Stockholm, taking the check and making reference to his co-inventor, J. Richardson Dewar. Dewar and Clark, Nobel Prize winners. No, "Clark and Dewar" sounded much better.

He thought again of what Audrey had said to him at the alumni dinner. She had summoned up a pitying smile as he lurched in, and sidled up beside him.

"Poor Ray!" she had said. "Come to see what a success your old lab partner has become?"

He'd stared at her balefully. "What the hell do you know about it?" he'd muttered.

"Oh, quite a lot," she trilled. "I watched Jamie pack your lab books the day he left the apartment."

She had waited for his reaction. He had not failed her.

"Why didn't you warn me?" he managed, eyes filling with self-pitying tears. "You knew it was both our work!"

"Oh, come, Ray dear! I didn't appreciate the significance until I came to Lockland. You do go on so about it that I finally realized it must be true. I'm coming, Don," she called, turning away. "It's that dreadful Ray Clark," he heard her saying to Don Benedict, linking her arm through his and clicking away on her high heels. "He's so hard to get away from without hurting his feelings!"

CHAPTER SEVENTEEN

Three days had passed since the débâcle of the anti-abortion rally. It should have gone well. They had had lovely weather, that holiday Monday. A clear blue sky, the welcome warmth of a beatific sun, the hedges' bursting buds, the large, tulip-shaped blossoms of the magnolias, all were reaffirmations of the rebirth of spring, symbolic of their cause. But the few staunch supporters of that cause treading their weary circle on the sidewalk outside the hospital, placards held less and less high, found very few candidates for their proselytizing.

Vanessa had felt sanctified by her sacred mission. Her placard proclaimed: "Four-month fetuses feel," an alliteration that had seemed profound on her kitchen linoleum, but had aroused no response from the visitors hurrying past them.

What had been planned as a silent vigil outside the main doors, the women's placards proclaiming a self-evident truth, had caused but a lackluster response. Their audience had been sparse. There had been few visitors to the hospital that Monday.

Vanessa was amazed that a holiday weekend could cause so many people to forget their sense of duty to sick relatives and friends. She always found time, in spite of working and caring for her family, to make regular visits to any neighbors who were hospitalized.

She had visited the neighborhood curmudgeon when he had had to have his hip pinned just last Friday. Although predictably, he had scowled at her and snarled "Go away! I'm too sick to see anyone!" she had stayed long enough to rearrange his room to make it more comfortable. She had even found a lovely vase for the flowers she had brought him. She accepted the fact that the old man was unable to express outwardly the inward gratitude he was feeling. His reticence did not bother her.

She still cringed inwardly, however, at the memory of the one woman she had accosted verbally during the protest. "Get out of my way, you fanatic," the woman had said with such venom that Vanessa could hardly bear to remember. "My son's in Intensive Care, stabbed by a teenage drug addict. Maybe that addict was a fetus that somebody like you saved. Why don't you crusade against drugs, you rich bitch in your silk dress."

Vanessa had looked down at her best blue shirtwaist dress. She had worn it to dignify the occasion, but it had clung damply to her hips in the relentless heat of high noon. She had felt a momentary qualm at the woman's cruel words, but she had gone on! She was proud of that. She had encouraged the girls to hold their placards high, and they had plodded on till afternoon visiting hours were over, pacing an oval that obstructed the people using the walk, forcing them to sidestep the solemn protest, or, for variety, marching single file back and forth along the sidewalk. She thought she could remember every crack in the cement.

A young teenager had delivered the ultimate humiliation. "Look at that front one," she had said, as if Vanessa could not hear. "The thin one with the blonde hair-do. Who does she remind you of? Oh, come on. You remember!" And when her friend proved uninterested, she said "I'll give you a hint! Watergate!" Her friend obediently studied the marching Vanessa a moment longer and said: "I give up! Rose Mary Woods?" and the little teenager, proud of her superiority, answered gleefully, "No, dummy, Pat Nixon! Richard Nixon's wife!" "Oh, her!" had been the disparaging response. Vanessa had felt like a specimen in a zoo.

Since then Vanessa had plummeted to earth. Her prayed-for miracle had appeared. She thought of her mother's words, spoken in the half-English, half-German bastard tongue that her family used.

"Vanessa," she would warn, "ask not your Gott for the miracle. For vielleicht it to you he gives!"

And now here was her miracle. But it was a miracle with a twist. Ray was definitely sober. Cold, determinedly, frighteningly sober. His habitual role of amiable drunk had only been a shield held up against the outside world anyway. Very few ever saw behind it to the depths of self-pity he delved into at home, when he was truly drunk, or knew how he depended on a morose detachment to guard against involvement in his home environment the rest of the time.

This new Ray was a Ray she had not seen before. Incisive, calculating, cruelly sarcastic when hindered, he was bound on a zealous mission that far exceeded any of her crusading attempts. Where she advertised her crusade, he hid his; where she had cohorts, he did battle alone; she wore her cause on her sleeve; this knight errant sported no lady's favor.

Vanessa sat at the kitchen table, her hands encircling her cup of tea. This new situation required clarification, if she were to deal with it. Something or somebody had, within the last week, forced Ray into sobriety. What had he learned?

She thought back. It started with convocation weekend. Ray had been drinking steadily all the week before. He had gone alone to the alumni dinner Friday night, and he had made a lot of noise coming home. He had wakened her with his shouts of farewell to the taxi driver. She had heard him staggering up the walk, complaining to the yews beside the front steps that they were obstructing him. He had stumbled on the front stairs; fumbled with the door key before he had come inside. When he had come to bed she had pretended to be asleep.

Yet she had remained awake after he had gone to sleep, because sleep had returned reluctantly. Usually, and she had just realized this, when he was truly drunk, he rolled over onto his back, a leaden weight, one arm outflung, the odor of metabolizing alcohol ebbing and flowing in synchronization with his snores. Friday night he had been restless, tossing and mumbling in his sleep, and crying out so that she could not return to sleep.

She was sure that his drunkenness the day of convocation was faked, as it so often was. Why, she wondered, had he decided to go to convocation? He hadn't been in years, since he had put on a ceremonial performance the year he had been refused promotion. Then he had been on a three-day bender of unparalleled proportions. This time was different.

Since Saturday he had abjured the bottle. An occasional glass of sherry, maybe, but she suspected the rye and gingerale he habitually carried around with him was mostly gingerale. Though of course she never knew where he hid his bottles. She had found them in clothes hampers, in with her pickles, out in the garage, or behind books in the study. But there had been no dead soldiers in the garbage since Saturday.

She should be exultant that what she had so devoutly wished for had come true. But Vanessa was wary. This sober Ray carried a secret, one that stemmed from Saturday. One that had had him out Tuesday, and Thursday night. One that brought him soberly home with his big, untidy briefcase crammed with papers. She occasionally had searched in there for a bottle, and it had never been locked. It was locked now.

Vanessa, in fact, was more than wary. Her large, china-blue eyes filled with tears. As she sipped her tepid tea she realized she was frightened. What had Ray seen and what did he know?

She thought of Audrey Benedict and how she had hated her. She had hated her for her assurance, her lack of consideration, her contempt for other people. She remembered how she had coaxed Ray to go to that cocktail party at the Faculty Club two years ago. She had searched the house for a week before for any hidden liquor. It was for that party she had splurged on that navy blue silk dress.

She shuddered, remembering. Ray had bowed low over Audrey's outstretched hand. "Madame Benedict," he'd proclaimed, "your beauty is as the sun." Vanessa had skittered in after him, mortified by his behavior. Privately she had hissed at him, but Ray had said "Cool it, 'Nessa! The lady loves it!" and proceeded directly to the bar. He had gotten royally drunk. She had floundered around, trying not to count his drinks, until she could take him home.

Even though Audrey was dead, Vanessa still hated her, for her death had dwarfed the protest into insignificance. She had not counted on that! Even in death Audrey was still interfering with Vanessa's ambitions!

Vanessa sensed that something connected with convocation had been responsible for the change in Ray, and she knew instinctively that it was not yet over. Ray had come home from convocation still in character, but even as he had told her of Audrey's death, there had been a kind of gloating. The gloating should have come from her, not him. And his sarcasm! That was new. He generally, as he often told her, reserved his erudition for someone more worthy of his steel. But he had dispensed it freely on that late Saturday afternoon, as if, joyously, he had a reason to live again.

Vanessa faced the future not with thanksgiving, but with dread.

CHAPTER EIGHTEEN

Grace, intending to walk, had started out early for her doctor's appointment at the hospital. It was another beautiful spring day. The sun was warm, the sky a cloudless blue. There was a soft breeze blowing. Birds chirped and rustled unseen in the lilac bushes on either side of the front steps. She turned her face up to the sun and smiled at the beauty of spring reborn. Her right hand grasped the iron railing for support as she walked carefully down the wide stone steps and along the stone path to the sidewalk. Clumps of spring flowers still lingered along the path. The fragrance of hyacinths, her mother's favorite flower, followed her footsteps. It was at times like this that she believed most fervently in the elemental force that some called God.

She strode along the sidewalk, spine straight, unencumbered arm swinging briskly, the heels of her sensible oxfords tapping out their message of self-sufficiency. She wore a conservative, heather tweed suit and a pale, mauve silk blouse. On her lapel nestled a twisted gold tangle set with Victorian amethysts. A triangular sling held her casted left arm close to her chest. Her thoughts frivolous, like the day, she marched past the house on the corner. Cracks showed through the stucco, black paint peeled from splintered window frames. A curtain hung unevenly from missing hooks behind the dusty glass. She wondered how the occupants would feel if one morning they woke up to find the grass cut, the lawn weeded, the old privet hedge trimmed, and perhaps even some geraniums beneath the front windows. Would they even notice? Poor souls, the weight of their inertia overwhelmed them. If only they didn't retain the strength to toss their beer bottles into the front yard.

The sturdy shoes went on, purposeful step echoing purposeful step. Past Margaret's Victorian brick, the glass of its high, narrow windows reflecting the budding trees. Margaret had taken off her storm windows! She, too, must be feeling the effects of spring. The polished brass Highlander, bagpipes at the ready, gleamed on the green front door. The low, stone wall surrounding the property was a delineator of Victorian rectitude. She saw the chaplain come down the front steps and waved a cheery greeting.

"Good morning, Mr. Davidson! Isn't it the most glorious day?"

"And a very good morning to you too, Dr. Grace! Aren't you out bright and early! Morning constitutional, is it?"

"Only insofar as I'm reconstituting my arm. Having my cast off today, I hope. It'll be nice to see my left wrist again. I've missed it. A frail thing, but mine own." Her wide smile beamed.

He walked down to the stone wall, and leaned against the column that formed one of the gateposts. He was wearing an old cardigan over his clerical-collared shirt.

"It's been a nuisance, hasn't it?" he commented. "I remember when I broke my wrist once, having to wear a cast for weeks. It was my writing arm and consequently my sermons were very short for six weeks."

An imp inside tempted her to say "God moves in mysterious ways!" but propriety restrained her. Instead she muttered an inconsequential rejoinder, waved goodbye and went quickly on.

She was to meet her doctor, Harold Day, in Emergency. A big, rotund bear of a man, he was the kind of no-nonsense doctor that Grace preferred. He had no small talk, his manner was direct, his voice brusque and his concern genuine. Grace liked to know the facts, and felt confident that if Harold couldn't handle a problem, his ego was secure enough that he would call in reinforcements. Colles' fractures of the wrist in seventy-year-old ladies was not, however, a problem he could not handle. He had probably dealt with more of them than many young orthopods.

She walked up the ramp past an ambulance, its back doors open, its cargo gone, and found him waiting for her just inside the double glass doors.

"Well, Grace, we'll just take you into the cast room down here and get this thing off," he said, escorting her down the hall, past the receptionist's desk, and some cubicles screened by white curtains, behind which she could hear fragments of conversation.

"Any desire to keep this as a souvenir?" he asked.

"I suppose you think I should prop it on the mantel!" replied Grace severely. "Is it supposed to remind me to be more careful next time?"

"You know I wouldn't dream of suggesting such a thing," Harold said. "Now just sit down on this stool here, and we'll use this nasty-looking instrument of torture to saw that thing off."

There was no conversation possible while the jagged-tooth circular saw whirred and vibrated through the plaster, revealing Grace's wrist for the first time in six weeks. It looked thinner and the muscles of her hand were wasted and attenuated. She rubbed it with her other hand.

"A bit stiff, I expect," remarked Dr. Day. "It'll come back the more you use it, but it wouldn't hurt you to have a few sessions in Physio to help you strengthen it." He went off to make the necessary arrangements.

A half hour later Grace, an appointment accommodatingly squeezed in between two others, was waiting on a bench along a corridor of the Physiotherapy department. She watched the people around her. She was never bored when she had others around her, because, like Andrew, she was an observer of the human condition.

A woman of around her own age, body shapeless under a flowered cotton house dress, thick ankles overflowing soft shoes with rundown heels, shuffled down the long corridor with the help of a four-legged chrome walker that she inched along laboriously in front of her. Grace wondered what her problem was.

"Poor soul, probably getting over a stroke," she thought.

Next to Grace on the bench slouched a tanned, muscled twenty-year-old, with light brown hair curling over his forehead, a determined jaw, and cheek creases that had been dimples in his childhood. He wore a faded, blue cotton, short-sleeved T-shirt and shorts. His long, muscular brown legs stretched far into the aisle in front of him, and a yellow Frisbee lay on the bench by his side.

She thought what a nice-looking boy he was. Head like that on an ancient Greek coin. She wondered idly who he was waiting for. Perhaps that was his grandmother, painfully making her way along the corridor. She heard a voice from a doorway call "Okay, Dave, you're next," and watched in some amusement as the boy beside her rose to his feet and disappeared into one of the rooms. Even perfect-looking bodies could have problems, evidently.

A trolley cart approached, bearing a coffee pot and cups. A volunteer, the initials "L.F.W.A." for "Lockland Faculty Wives' Association" entwined on the pocket of the blue smock, bent solicitously over her and asked her if she would care for some coffee? Perhaps a simple little magazine to read? They had the latest edition of *T.V. Guide* or perhaps she would enjoy *Woman's Home Companion*?

A spirit of pure devilment (brought on, she reflected afterwards, by the spring day, her freed wrist, and her own erroneous assumptions) made her answer ambiguously.

"No, thank you," she replied. "I never read magazines."

The volunteer's expression did not change. She retreated briefly, only to reappear with an unsought cup of tea, which she placed gently in Grace's right hand. She bestowed a sweet smile on Grace, as if she were dealing with a slightly retarded child, and then, not bothering to move the cart farther down the hall, continued her conversation with her fellow worker in hushed tones. They must assume that those who don't read can't hear, thought Grace, listening unashamedly.

"They've been asking questions all over the hospital. They even went down to Pharmacy to check all their records. I heard they don't know where it came from."

"Gary says they've been to the university as well, checking in the laboratories. Well, he's in Chemistry, and they've certainly been there. They tried to talk to Ray Clark, but he was sodden, positively sodden. He's worse this week than he has ever been! I don't know why they tolerate him."

"Anyway, they say she was killed by an anaesthetic. The first place they went here was to the Operating Rooms. All the operations were late, because they were checking over the supplies in the cupboards. You should have heard the Head Nurse complain!"

"I heard that if they found where it came from, they'd know who killed her."

"Miriam says they suspect one of the anaesthetists. They say he's been having trouble at home, and somebody saw him downtown just last week with Audrey Benedict, having coffee at Dinty's."

"I heard that she was flirting with the man who was to address convocation at the dinner on the Friday night. Whatever she was saying must have been something else, because Dr. Dewar turned bright red. You could see he was upset!"

"Honestly! I don't know how Don Benedict put up with it! It just makes me sick to think that he was hood-winked for all his married life!"

"Well, you couldn't tell him anything. He thought she was wonderful!"

"I'm not so sure he felt like that lately. My husband went

to a meeting with him in Hamilton recently, and something he said to Elmer made Elmer think that he was getting pretty fed up with her shenanigans. Elmer came home and told me that Audrey Benedict had better watch her step!"

"Well, obviously she didn't!"

"They still haven't found out where the poison came from, though, because they're still searching for it. I know yesterday they went to Maternity, and nobody would talk to them just then because they were delivering premature twins. So they went back today. Agnes told me. It wasn't her day to work, but Jane's on holidays."

"Eve was telling me that Helen won't talk about it at all. You know she discovered the body? You didn't? She sat right next to her during the whole ceremony! You knew they hadn't spoken since "that" day, and then when she didn't move, Helen actually had to ask her to get up?"

"Wasn't she dead already, then?"

"Yes, so at least she didn't hear Helen make the first move. She didn't twitch a muscle, and Helen looked down at her and she was dead."

"I wonder if she feels guilty that she never spoke to her after that meeting."

"I don't see why she should. I wouldn't. I mean, the fact that she's dead doesn't change how poisonous . . . oooh! I mean, how awful she was when she was alive. Think what trouble her article caused us. I think she was a vicious. . ."

"Oh, look, here come some new people. Is the coffee still hot?"

The cart drifted farther up the hall, out of earshot. Grace put her teacup down beside her, and gazed thoughtfully into space. There were few secrets in a hospital, she reflected. How difficult to separate fact from fancy, embroidery from simple stitchery.

"Dr. Forrester?" The question came from a young woman in her navy Physiotherapy uniform, standing in a doorway down the hall. Grace rose from her seat, and faintly smiling, sailed past the two volunteers staring at her.

CHAPTER NINETEEN

James Dewar shot his cuffs below the sleeves of his dark blue business suit as he walked briskly up the wide stone steps of Harvey Hall. The stone balustrades curved away to frame the symmetrical double oak doors of the central entrance. Even more than the name chiseled above, or the bronze dedication plaque just inside with the names of benefactors etched in Old English script, those doors represented authority. Grasping the twisted bronze handles to swing the massive doors open on their smoothly oiled mechanism, one felt that just so would one have to deal with the world behind those doors, where massive authority, vested in titles, was able to resist those who did not know how to oil the mechanism of administration. James Dewar had no such fears. He had come a long way from the unsure undergraduate who had dealt with administration in this building's predecessor, a temporary building set behind the heating plant. Harvey Hall, large, three-storied, latticed windows set in ivied red brick, surrounded by close-clipped lawns, was quadruple the size of the old building.

James Dewar imagined the administrative staff had quadrupled too. It was axiomatic in the business world that, as there was more money to spend, more administrators were there to control its expenditure. He did not expect it to be different in the academic world.

He, himself, now had an administrative assistant.

Thelma was a tall, asexual-looking woman in her mid-thirties. She wore plain dark skirts and tweed jackets, large wire glasses, and kept her dull blonde hair parted smoothly in the middle and swept back in a bun at the nape of her neck. She certainly showed no interest in James Dewar except as a scientist, beset by all the foibles that creative men had. Quiet, efficient, she oversaw the various secretaries that came and went in the outer office, arranged schedules, appointments and traveling plans, briefed him as needed on matters which he should know, and turned a blind eye to Jamie Dewar's extra-curricular pursuits.

Of course, Jamie had tried to interest the admirable Thelma when she had first been hired. It was a matter of form for him to attach his female employees to him with his charm. This time, however, his approaches had been half-hearted, Thelma being distant, rather boyish in figure, studiously uninterested, and slightly disdainful. The blunted arrows of his advances glanced harmlessly off the shield of her indifference, and once he had explained to himself that this must spring from her asexuality, the two of them functioned as an efficient duo in his business world.

Jamie gave little thought to Thelma's life outside office hours. He imagined, on the rare occasions when he spared the time to think about it, that she had sprung from two parents in the usual way, and that she probably returned to them each evening. Or, if, she was on her own, that she climbed the stairs to some solitary apartment where she knitted long scarfs, or collected stamps or goldfish. He would not have believed, if anyone could have told him, that Thelma had been the other woman in his bank president's life for many years.

He walked through the front doors into the marble foyer, and on to the information office. With a winning smile for the receptionist seated behind the counter, he said, "I'm Dr. Dewar. I believe I'm expected in the President's office?"

She rose to greet him. "Yes, Dr. Dewar. They're waiting for you. Right this way."

At least the meeting was on neutral ground. He could not imagine having to converse with the police at the old homestead, surrounded by the skeptical glances of his relatives, nor had he any intention of going to the police station like a common criminal. President Regan had sounded embarrassed when he had called. He should be. To give in so spinelessly to someone's persuasion showed a sad lack of character. Well, that trait could be turned to his advantage. Obviously, Dr. Forrester had talked. What, he wondered, did they know? Did they know more than that he had known Audrey in New York? Would they believe that his meeting with her in the maze on Saturday morning had been accidental? He wondered what explanation Audrey had given the old stick she'd married for leaving so early Saturday morning? He should have asked her what she'd said. 'Course, who would have thought that might be important? So long as the other business hadn't come out.

He wondered also to whom else the police had spoken. Were there others out there, unseen, who posed a threat? In life there were always a few people who would be delighted to receive delicate information. His career could be ruined. He would have to play the next hour or so very cautiously. He felt the surge of adrenaline in his veins. Nobody was going to get James Dewar, not at this stage, not with all there was to lose.

"Never underestimate your opposition!" he reminded himself. He himself was living proof that small towns occasionally held brilliant minds. A university community abounded with people with native intelligence.

"Treat this as you would an oral examination. You hold all the cards. Play with them. They're forced to question the guest speaker at convocation. They daren't make it an interrogation. They have to pretend it's just a meeting in the administrative offices. You're not even under oath." A judicious lie, when absolutely safe, was not against Dewar's moral code. You played by hard rules in his league.

The receptionist ushered him into a comfortable conference room. Corduroy-covered chairs in autumn colors stood against walls paneled in warm mahogany. President Regan rose to shake his hand and introduce him to the other men who had stood up as he entered. He shook hands with the Dean of the Law faculty, a small, rabbity man with thinning hair, and a colorless, paunchy man in a beige suit, who was from the Police Department. "Name's Merritt," the man said jovially, smiling with thin lips. James Dewar's eyes scanned the room. A middle-aged woman, in a blue skirt and cardigan, notebook poised, sat back unobtrusively to take notes. How old fashioned. No tape recorder.

The president spoke. "Merritt here would just like to ask you some questions about the late Mrs. Benedict. It appears you may have been one of the last people to see her, and since the police are anxious to find out more about how she was on that Saturday morning, we've arranged this little meeting. Of course, you understand our concern that you are being put to this inconvenience. We are very grateful that you were able to find the time in your busy schedule to come here."

A graceful speech by the president setting the stage for the questions that must inevitably follow. "Marches very trippingly off the tongue," thought James.

Dave Merritt took up the slack. "Thank you, President Regan. Now, Dr. Dewar, we are anxious to get a little bit of background information. For example, how long ago did you know Mrs. Benedict, when and where did you first meet her, had you kept in touch since? That sort of thing." Dave Merritt smiled benignly. He looked as if he dealt mostly with such crimes as car theft.

"Certainly, Mr. — ah, Merritt, did you say your name was? Well, I'm afraid I'm not going to be of much help to you." Dewar heaved a patient sigh. "I knew Mrs. Benedict many years ago in New York, as I believe you are aware, when I was just a graduate student. She and I attended the same university. We were, of course, not in the same field. I believe I encountered her mainly because we must have lived in the same general vicinity" (no one need know just how near) "and often took the same public transportation to school." He shrugged. "I suspect we were even at some of the same social functions. I certainly knew her well enough to remember her when she came up to me at the alumni dinner Friday night to reintroduce herself to me. Though I doubt very much if I'd have remembered her name if she hadn't jogged my memory! I hate to admit it but these faces from the past do change with time! It's been quite a while since I was a graduate student."

"So you hadn't seen her since your student days?"

"No, I'm sure I haven't. I didn't even know her by her married name. To me she'd been little Audrey Follows. I would have been unlikely to run into her once I began working, since she was not a scientist. I believe her degree was in the Humanities."

"Did you have much of an opportunity to talk to her at the dinner, Dr. Dewar?"

"Well, I think we exchanged pleasantries. I was rather amused at the coincidence of meeting her here at my old Alma Mater. She told me she'd married one of the faculty members, and was now a housewife. My memories from my New York days would suggest that's what she'd always wanted to be — a simple housewife. No great career ambitions. Women of that generation generally went to university hoping to get a man." He smiled at his audience. "Used to 'come out' the generation before that. Stated their intentions a little more blatantly, then. I suspect many of the girls at university now, though, really want their degree," he added generously.

A silence ensued. President Regan seemed slightly embarrassed by the questioning, low-key though it was. He certainly took no active part in the conversation. The unobtrusive little man from the Law faculty peered with his pinkish eyes at the two protagonists but did not speak. Dave Merritt seemed preoccupied by a doodle on the pad in front of him. James Dewar broke the awkward stillness.

"As a matter of fact, I do recall that Mrs. Benedict was very keen on reminiscing about the olden days in New York."

"Oh," said Dave softly. "What was she reminiscing about?"

"Nothing much in particular. The cost of food when we were both poor, the long ride in to the university. Little events she recalled. Nothing very specific."

He'd better watch that. One should make it a rule never to volunteer information. Not unless you were leading the conversation into the channels you wanted it to go. He knew that ploy well from thesis orals. But this time, better let them make the first move. He began to twist his signet ring around on his little finger.

"Did you have much in common during those long-ago days, Dr. Dewar?"

He bristled. "What are you insinuating, Mr. Merritt?"

"Nothing, Dr. Dewar. You mentioned that you discussed the price of food, and that you lived in the same general neighborhood, so I was just wondering if you were similarly circumstanced during that period of your lives?"

"I'm sorry. Actually, if you knew about academic life, you'd realize that she was just an undergraduate at the time, while I was a graduate student. We were also in different disciplines. Since I can barely recall her, I suspect our meetings were purely social. I must say, she hasn't occupied a large portion of my conscious mind during the intervening years. However, I was certainly prepared to be polite when I met her again. She came running up to me at the dinner, like a friendly little puppy, and, *noblesse oblige*, you know."

The president made a small moue of distaste. The rabbity man pressed back uncomfortably against his chair back. The secretary recrossed her legs, and sat, pencil poised. Dave Merritt seemed unsure about how to proceed.

"Did you plan then on meeting the next morning, Dr. Dewar, or was your meeting this time with Mrs. Benedict also a coincidence?" he inquired, doodling on his pad with an air of embarrassment.

James Dewar eyed him narrowly. "It would be quite unseemly for the main speaker at graduation to spend the time before the ceremonies keeping an assignation with a married woman he barely knew, Mr. Merritt," he said. "I assure you that I was merely trying to clear my head after making some last-minute revisions to my address when we met. In fact, you might say that when I was deep in thought, I was accosted — I can describe it as nothing else — by the same woman whom I had had to be pleasant to the evening before."

"What did she want?"

He felt his heartbeat quicken. Better go slowly on this one, James, he thought. He hesitated while he marshaled his thoughts.

"I'm not quite sure. She came gushing up to me, saying how remarkable it was to see me so soon again, and wishing me luck in my speech that afternoon. She said how much she was looking forward to hearing it. The usual kind of thing that women say. I didn't take much notice."

"How long did you talk, Dr. Dewar?"

He became vaguely irritated. When would this inane line of questioning end? He had given a perfectly adequate explanation.

"Well, I wasn't clocking time during our conversation. Perhaps fifteen minutes. She certainly loved to talk. I was anxious to get away, but common politeness. . . ."

"Do you remember what she was wearing at the time?" The questions kept coming, small pellets from an air gun, meant to hurt but not to kill.

"Bright yellow, a yellow dress, I believe."

He knew it was yellow, and he knew why she had chosen that color. He had told her once that she looked best in yellow. She had redone their entire apartment in yellow after he said that. That was only a short time before they'd broken up. The long yellow drapes had been the backdrop for a different coupling one afternoon. . . . Had she ever let that slip?

He wrenched his mind back to the present. He looked at the paunchy plainclothesman, sandy hair combed off the broad peasant forehead. He twisted his ring. Why wouldn't the simpleton look him in the eye?

"Must you keep doodling?" he said suddenly, almost without volition.

"I'm so sorry, sir," said Dave, smiling apologetically. "Didn't realize it would bother you. It's just a habit of mine. Helps me think." He put down his pen.

"Oh, it doesn't matter," said James Dewar irritably. "Certainly, if it helps you think, continue. Perhaps we can get this over with more quickly!"

"Did Mrs. Benedict have a camera, sir, when she was with you in the gardens?"

"I don't know," said Jamie, honestly bewildered. Why would she have brought a camera to talk to him? Had she kept it in her big shoulder purse? "I don't remember seeing one. Though she may have had one in her purse. I honestly don't know."

"Did Mrs. Benedict seem upset or nervous? Did she mention having to meet anyone else?"

Audrey had certainly not been nervous. She thrived on others' misfortunes; she fed on human misery; she got excited by danger. But you couldn't say that. She had stated her terms baldly, quietly, pleasantly. He could hear her now, the raspy voice lowered to a whisper.

"It's not much fun trying to live on a university professor's salary, Jamie. It's not like the money you're making. I've heard about the patent on 'Donerin,' you see. There's an old acquaintance from our past you might remember. Ray Clark. He's an alcoholic now. He does seem to have a lot of knowledge about 'Donerin.' Not that he could ever do anything! You needn't worry about him. But he did tell me how much that patent is worth."

"So . . . I wondered if you'd care to make a charitable

donation to an academic life, Jamie? Not the kind you could take off your income tax, unfortunately. That would be so much better, wouldn't it? But then, consider it a personal gesture. For old times' sake. Now J. Richardson Dewar wouldn't want it known that he had homosexual interests, would he? Especially since he's so acclaimed as a great heterosexual lover! Your world's not ready for that, is it?"

"Was it just a one-time affair, Jamie, that day I came home early from class and found you with that professor? Or does expediency motivate you still? Yes, I still remember, names and everything. I've often wondered what your specific motivation was then. Did it have to do with marks, I wonder? The world does thrive on scandal! I imagine the board of your firm would be quite shocked! Even this late it would be almost worth telling just to see the reaction! No? You don't seem thrilled! So, perhaps an anonymous donation instead? Nothing too extensive. Monthly, I think. Naturally a box-office number would be best. . . ."

He could feel himself flushing. He felt the same surge of anger, the gorge rising in his throat, as it had when Audrey Benedict had tried to blackmail him. He fought it down. He must answer quietly. Here was the minefield. He must pick his way through it. Caution, Jamie, caution.

"No, she wasn't nervous. She was restrained, quiet, deferential."

"Did she tell you what she was going to do next, Dr. Dewar?" No, not that day. Just a steady bleeding for the rest of his life.

His body tensed. "No, we talked for a few minutes, as I said, and I went back to my room to finish my address, and get ready for the ceremonies." And to think about blackmail, and the General, and how her plans would affect Jamie's future. She had gone off with a wave of her hand, promising to be at convocation that afternoon and cheer him on mentally.

"She did say how much she was looking forward to that afternoon's events. We said goodbye, and she waved, and went down the path to the North Street exit."

Merritt seemed uncertain as to whether or not to continue, and looked at the president, who said, formally, "Thank you for your time, Dr. Dewar." They stood and shook hands all round. The secretary remained seated, pencil at long last at rest.

He turned to leave. "I wish I could have been of more help in this distressing circumstance. No, no trouble at all, really. Glad to oblige." He mouthed all the conventional phrases, refused the proferred coffee and left. In his mind there was just one thought — a disturbing thought. Could she have left evidence? The General would not tolerate any sign of deviance in his firm. He abhorred it. Thundered around about Sodom and Gomorrah! Great Christ in the sky! Had her purse contained a tape recorder? Where was her purse now? Did the police have it? Did anyone know what she had said? Had she had a chance to talk? Damn her anyway! She deserved everything that had happened to her.

CHAPTER TWENTY

The old, leather-topped desk with the faded gold scrolls was placed near enough to the window so that the chaplain, glancing up from his papers, could see the pavement leading to the entrance to Harvey Hall. He had watched J. Richardson Dewar stride assuredly towards the stone steps a short time earlier, and he had waited, bemused, until a subdued James Dewar retraced his steps, and turning right, disappeared from view behind the Chemistry building. The change in his mien had been striking, and it upset the man watching from above.

Michael Davidson had counseled students for many years, but he had never really thought about body language before, at least, not on a conscious level. But a good counselor subconsciously takes note of his subject's attitude: the erect posture of the confident man, the telltale avoidance of eyes meeting when a topic that might disturb equilibrium is first broached, the flush of the unaccustomed liar. And Michael Davidson was a good counselor. He had picked up those non-verbal clues over the years and relied on his perception to help him help others. But the change in attitude had seldom struck him as forcibly as it did right now, watching James Dewar, presuming himself unobserved, slowly sag like an old tire leaking air.

He wondered if he could write a sermon about body language. The Last Supper, Judas and Simon Peter, the contrast between the two, one adoring, one deceiving. . . . Did the non-verbal clues show Jesus the betrayer? He would bring in how material possessions, the putting on of ceremonial finery, would not deceive the discerning eye. The man inside shone through to reveal himself in unspoken ways. Of course, there were exceptions. A psychopath, without moral fiber, seeing nothing wrong in his behavior, would not give himself away. He could be trapped only by the evidence of others. He did not think that Judas had been a psychopath.

He paused suddenly, and rested his forehead on his hand, his elbow marking one of the scrolls that bordered the desk top. Why would J. Richardson Dewar leave so dispiritedly? What had they said to him? What questions had the police posed to the principal speaker at spring convocation? What innuendos had destroyed the confidence of such a worldly man?

His eyes unseeing, he had looked downward, his shoulders slumping, his body language unwittingly expressing his distress. It was a shameful day when vile criminal acts debased the climax of the university year! Would Lockland ever live down the events of the last five days? The chaplain shook his head sadly. Destroyed, all destroyed! The solemnity of the ceremony, the meaningfulness of the benediction, God's blessing on those young lives emerging into the world from the protection of their Alma Mater, all besmirched by the stain that lay around the feet of those whom the university had chosen to honor. The living symbol of attainment degraded by vulgar doings, vulgar sayings, cheap, common gossip. The Reverend Michael Davidson was under no illusion. This convocation would be remembered only as the one at which someone in the audience had been murdered during the ceremony, and the Honorary Graduand subsequently questioned. Rumor might even label him a suspect!

And all because of that woman: a gaudy carapace of a woman, untouched by the Christian spirit. Unfit to be a member of the university community. Vindictive and devoid of charity. She had advocated killing, and in return had herself been killed. Oh, how the thought had been father to the deed!

Yet, one should not forget that she, too, was one of God's creatures. One could, however, presume she was one of the lesser ones, a discredit to those nobler members of her sex who strove to uphold the ideals of womankind. Not that he was one to feel that all women should remain at the hearthside. He bethought himself of Joan of Arc, leading her followers into battle, Florence Nightingale, that heroine of Scutari, Mother Teresa, in the slums of Calcutta. Wasn't it interesting? None of these historic examples was married! Certainly Audrey Benedict was not of their ilk. Nor was she one of the many caring women he knew and admired. It was, indeed, one of God's more inscrutable acts that had placed such a person at this seat of higher learning.

He wondered if anyone had a right to kill? In self-defense, of course! Society condoned that. Society also condoned killing for the greater good. So were wars justified, executions explained, inquisitions conducted. Killing in its various guises had been ceremonially enshrined throughout history. But how could one justify Audrey's macabre death? Had her killer known how she would suffer? Margaret had told him exactly how Audrey had died. It had been a martyr's death: she'd been conscious throughout, unable by stages to move, then to speak, and finally, at last, to breathe. So that she had suffocated silently, able till the last to hear, to understand, to wait until a lack of oxygen brought the release of oblivion and death.

His thoughts were in turmoil, tumbling around and around in his brain as if seeking a way out of the puzzle. When did she die? Was it during that stirring exhortation to the graduates that J. Richardson Dewar had given? She had evidently known him in the past. Did his voice at the end give her peace, or impotent fury that she could not move, call for help, even open her lids and see?

Perhaps she had breathed her last during the benediction. If it had been necessary for her to die in that
grotesque way, would it not have been some comfort to be
sent to answer to that Higher Power with the familiar
phrase: "And may the Peace of God, and the Love that
passes all understanding, be with you now . . ."? To die in a
state of grace? Was that so bad?

The pedestrians on the sidewalk outside his window
passed by unseen. His thoughts swung to Don Benedict.
His suffering, so evident, came from loving too well, if not
wisely. A common fault! Though surely love was never
wrong, just misguided. He could think of examples where
love had led to great unhappiness for those who were not
loved in return. For human love, unlike God's, is imperfect.
Don himself, by his loving kindnesses, would have brought
joy to Audrey, and there was no gainsaying it, she had once
brought joy to him. "They are none so blind as they who
will not see!" Don had been impervious to her faults. At
fault himself, he had perceived her faults as virtues. With
knowledge would come disillusionment. So, for his sake,
could anybody now not pretend?

The chaplain passed his frail, veined hands wearily over
his eyes. His thoughts were muddled, edged round by
sayings. But his duty now became clear. He would conduct
the memorial service with all the dignity and ritual he could
muster to help comfort Don Benedict. He could do no less.
Don must never suspect that others knew his wife had been
less than perfect.

But what of his other duty — Lockland? His university
lay bleeding, shot through by the arrows of rumor and
innuendo, sullied by the scandal of murder done, and
demeaned by the need to invade the privacy and dignity of
her staff and honored guests.

He straightened in his chair. One could see him don his
mental armor. For the sake of Lockland, the rumors must
be laid to rest. The entire resources of the university must
be mobilized to find a culprit and thus restore equilibrium.

Only so could Lockland rise above the calumny, free again. And, he had to admit, with Audrey Benedict's malicious influence no longer bringing unrest to the university community.

He placed his palms on the edge of his desk to help him rise. He was weary these days. He felt so old. It was time to go home. Margaret would be expecting him. He wished he had been able to work. There on the desk lay a letter from a young undergraduate, looking for a summer job and hoping that the chaplain, with his knowledge of the alumni, could help her. A request from a recent graduate, asking him to officiate at his daughter's baptism, needed answering right away. Ordinarily, he loved baptisms. Another lamb in the fold! He could not bring himself in his present state to even answer his mail.

He stood beside his desk, his mind wandering timidly down unfamiliar streets. Work was the salve of the human spirit. In work there is forgetfulness, self-respect, fulfillment. He thought how unhappy the people on welfare must be, wandering through each dreary day without the balm of distracting work. In work he should be able to put death aside. Death was a familiar face to him. He did not fear its sightless eyes. Beyond them lay the glory of God, and in that he believed utterly. But murder was different. He had never had to stare at the bloody mask of murder before. Would whoever skulked behind it be unmasked?

He looked a tired, frail old man. Audrey's silent, secret murder dabbed at his mind with cottony wisps of uncertainty, held with bony fingers, to poison his ease, soak up his peace of mind. He could find no release in work. His mind circled in a diminishing spiral. The nature of her dying haunted him — that creeping death. Even for the greater good, did anyone deserve to die in such a manner?

CHAPTER TWENTY-ONE

"I knew her," she said simply. "I knew her and I hated her. She was no friend of mine. I wouldn't have sat near her at my son's graduation if you paid me!" She laughed ironically. "And that's funny, too!"

She leaned back comfortably in her chair and put her feet up on the footstool. She appeared very relaxed, sitting on her sunny patio, a cool drink of iced tea in her hand. She was an elegant-looking woman in her mid-forties, tall, slim, intelligent, with the sophistication that went with old money.

"She'd been blackmailing me for years, you know," she went on conversationally, as if she were telling a rather routine story. "It's ironic she died last weekend, of course. I finally met up with her again Friday night at the alumni dinner. She reminded me of a — how shall I put it, an old snake." She swirled the ice in her drink reflectively. "Dry-skinned, ready to strike, hissing and rattling, but she no longer had any fangs. I told her face to face that I was through paying. It gave me immeasurable pleasure to tell her personally! She didn't take it very well." Alison shrugged. "But what could she do? My husband has died, and my children are mature enough to understand. In this day and age, it wouldn't seem important to them. So you see I'm finally a free woman!" She smiled at the detective, sitting opposite her and staring incredulously at her.

"You think I've got a super motive, don't you?" she went on in her soft, slightly husky voice. "I haven't! I didn't need to kill her, you see. Her hold on me was over last weekend, if not a year ago."

"Could you tell me why, Mrs. Backstrom?" asked Bill cautiously. "Why had she had a hold on you?"

"I had an illegitimate baby once, years ago," she said sadly, "when those things mattered. She found out and threatened to tell my husband. I've been paying her for years. And when my husband died a year ago, I kept on for a while, because" — she hesitated for a moment — "I suppose it was a habit, and it wasn't uppermost in my mind after I lost Richard. And, to be truthful, the sudden cessation of what I had said was support of an old aunt would have looked peculiar while we were settling Richard's estate." She smiled serenely, "I finally decided that the time had come to put an end to the nonsense."

Bill wriggled uncomfortably on the webbing of his chair. "How did she find out about the baby, Mrs. Backstrom?" he asked.

She sighed. "Life is full of coincidences, Detective Barnes," she remarked. "She was evidently living with the man who was the father of my baby, and he must have told her. She appeared on my doorstep one morning, just after my husband had gone to work, asked herself in and told me she knew about my indiscretion while at college. I paid her out of my allowance for years! Then she wanted more. They always do, I'm told. So I invented my Aunt Myrtle. My parents were dead by then and couldn't deny an Aunt Myrtle. My husband was very family oriented. He was happy to contribute to my old aunt's support. I never told him the truth. He was an old-fashioned man. It would have destroyed him."

"How long had this blackmail been going on?"

"Oh, I'd been married for two years, had my first son when she arrived on the scene. He was only three months old, and I was young and unsure of myself. She upped the ante over the years. She knew I had married into a very wealthy family. My husband comes from an old business family in the New York area, and I suppose it seemed to the baby's father faintly amusing that I managed to rise from the financial depths where he left me, to marry rather well. He must have read about my marriage in a society column somewhere. So he told her all about me! God, he really was a louse! This weekend brought it all back! He might be the smartest thing on two legs, but my husband had it all over him for kindness and decency. I could never have hurt Richard!" she explained. "So, instead, I paid that bitch for years."

"I'm sorry, you've left me behind!" exclaimed Bill, trying desperately to keep up with the he's and she's in the conversation. "Who's the smartest thing on two legs?"

"Jamie Dewar, of course!" she explained. "He's the great guy who got me pregnant in my first year at Lockland. We boarded in the same house. He swore undying love until I told him I was pregnant. Then he disappeared for the summer, into the bush. If it hadn't been for Margaret McDuff, I think I would have died. My kindly landlady threw me out when she found out I was pregnant. I didn't dare go home and tell my parents! They were so proud that they had a daughter at college! So I told them I had a job, and Margaret took me in and I had my little girl and gave her up." She looked stricken for a moment, then lit a cigarette and took a meditative puff before continuing.

"I met Richard at a meeting during my final year. He had graduated from a U.S. university five years before, and by then was working his way up in the family business. We fell in love and got married, but I never found the right moment to tell him about my baby. And then that woman appeared on the doorstep, and after that, there was no right time. So I paid."

"So you're saying that Dr. Dewar was the father of your baby, and told Mrs. Benedict about it years ago?" repeated Bill. "And she's blackmailed you ever since?"

"Uh-huh," replied Alison Backstrom. "That's right. But when I was formally introduced to her on the Friday night at the alumni dinner, I suddenly knew that it was the very time and place to destroy her little pretensions. She had no suspicion I'd be there. I've only been a trustee since Richard died. I certainly didn't expect to see her there. I had planned on calling her sometime later that weekend. Very funny, you know!" She went on contemplatively. "Audrey there as a Dean's wife; Jamie Dewar, the cause of it all, there as guest speaker; and I, as a trustee. I didn't go near Jamie, of course. I'd as soon speak to Satan himself, but it gave me great pleasure to tell Audrey face to face that we had nothing in common any more."

"What did she say?" asked Bill, fascinated.

"She was rather taken aback, I think, especially since I spoke to her there at the dinner. She must have been struck by the incongruity of it, I suspect. Dean's wife introduced to trustee. Trustee recognizes her blackmailer and promptly tells her she is not submitting to any more blackmail." A weary, pained look appeared on Alison's beautiful face. "And then the chaplain launched into 'Vengeance is mine'!" she said wryly. "It was like a morality play!"

"Did you never worry that when you came back to Lockland as a trustee someone would remember you as an undergraduate and repeat what had happened then?" asked Bill.

"Not really! It didn't much matter after Richard died," she replied. "He was the only one I really wanted to protect. Besides, I had no choice. My family and friends would not have understood why I wouldn't be a trustee. I'm not the shrinking-violet type, you see." She laughed. "Also, you have to remember that was many years ago and I don't use my former name. No one would have expected Alison Backstrom from New York State to be that little innocent from a farming hamlet who had been so foolish. I can hardly picture her myself!"

"Did you say that James Dewar and Audrey Benedict

lived together?" repeated Bill, trying to get a handle on the incredible story he was hearing.

"So she said," replied Alison, "and although she wasn't anyone you could trust, I don't know why she'd lie about that. She must certainly have known him reasonably well, unless he boasted about his conquests to mere acquaintances. This all happened when she was living in New York, because I first had to send the checks to an address in New York, then to Toronto, and finally to Marlburg."

"So she was a blackmailer!" repeated Bill almost to himself. "I wonder who else she blackmailed?"

"She didn't indulge in those kind of confessions with her victims, as far as I know," answered Alison gently. "Why don't you ask the good Dr. Dewar? Perhaps she had a hold on him, as well. I don't think they stayed together after New York, because I know she was working in Toronto two or three years after she started blackmailing me!"

"I wonder what she would have had on him?" mused Bill.

"I couldn't begin to guess," she replied. "If you had ever met my husband, you would realize that James Dewar is not capable of being a gentleman, but whether he ever did anything that she could bleed him for I wouldn't know. He is such a glib talker! It would be hard to see how he could have made a mistake he couldn't wriggle out of!" She hesitated for a moment, thinking.

"'Course, I can't help wondering. . . ." She stopped and looked at Bill, consideringly.

"Yes?"

"Dr. Dewar was gone for quite a few minutes while the procession was being formed. Right before we were to march in. Of course, we all had to wait in line till he came back. He was to walk in right behind President Regan. I think the man who had arranged us in order was getting a little annoyed. We, of course, just presumed Dr. Dewar had gone to the washroom. It was unlike Jamie Dewar to be nervous . . . and you did say she was killed before the ceremony. . . ." She faltered to a stop and looked at Bill to see his reaction. Bill hastily averted his eyes to write a few words in his notebook. What was she implying? Could Dr. Dewar have kept an entire processional waiting while he murdered Audrey Benedict?

He thought he would leave her suggestion for Dave Merritt to follow up. He had done his bit figuring out that Alison Backstrom, Trustee, could be the unknown Alice, the trustee's wife at the alumni dinner, that Don Benedict had told them about. Bill had been mentally rehearsing the back-patting explanation of his cleverness to Merritt all the while he had been talking to Mrs. Backstrom. That is, until she had tossed that one rotten apple into the barrel of his complacency. The worm of insinuation had peeked its head out momentarily, and now the apple lay there for him to pick up.

Yup, he thought, this one I leave for Dave.

"Could I ask where you stayed last weekend?" asked Bill, finally looking up. It was time he got down to the more mundane details he had been sent to find out.

"With the president and his wife, of course," said Alison, vouchsafing no more information. She was not quite sure if her innuendo about Dewar had been noted. "We've been friends for years."

"And you sat where?" persisted Bill.

"You mean at convocation, I gather," she said with an amused smile. "I think President Regan can account for my movements until we gathered with the other trustees in the Oak Room before the ceremonies. And then I went in the procession and sat with the other trustees. I could hardly bear to listen to Jamie Dewar preach to the graduates. What a hypocrite! The price we pay for being trustees!"

She laughed. "It's worse for Frank Regan, of course, and the chancellor. They have to attend all sorts of ceremonies. We trustees are only expected to appear at convocation."

"Did you see Mrs. Benedict at graduation at all?" he asked.

"Neither dead or alive," she answered cheerfully. "I only

met her twice in my life. On my doorstep long ago, and when I was introduced to her Friday night. 'Course I had to change the payee on my checks to Benedict three years ago, so I knew she was married and here in Marlburg."

She became decisive. "I assure you, dear sir, that my telling her personally, during a formal alumni dinner, that her reign of blackmail was over, was the only mischievous thing I did the entire weekend! But I must also confess that I enjoyed doing it immensely!"

She rose dismissively to her feet and held out her hand, obviously terminating the interview. Bill decided to accept her decision for the present. He had a great deal of information to digest, and there were some rather startling things that he wanted to discuss with Dave. Like Dr. Dewar's absence from the procession, and the blackmail! What a fantastic story! And Mrs. Benedict had told her husband that Alison Backstrom was her friend! He closed his notebook. They chatted pleasantly about inconsequential matters as she led him to the front door and ushered him out to the street.

Alison walked back through the hall into the sunny kitchen and put down her glass on the counter near the dishwasher. There was a knot in her stomach, that had not been there for some time.

She thought about her conversation with the detective and how she had been forced to submerge the old, familiar feelings that had welled up, just as she had had to do with Richard for most of her married life. Richard had once seen her looking pensively at pictures of little girls in smocked dresses, and she braced herself as she remembered how he had come over to her smilingly and said, "Three boys are pretty special, Allie. I'm sorry I couldn't give you the daughter you wanted. Shall we see if we can adopt a little girl?" She had almost broken down then and told him. It had taken all her resolve to close the magazine, smile brightly at him and say, "Richard, I would rather have your boys than anyone else's girls!" He had seemed satisfied by that. Later, he had teased her occasionally about not being able to dress the boys in frilly clothes.

Tears started to her eyes and she brushed them impatiently away. She made an abrupt turn into the library and deliberately poured herself a stiff scotch. She turned on the stereo. Linda Ronstadt singing "When Your Lover Has Gone" filled the room. She sank back into her husband's old leather chair and took a large swallow. The music sent a chill creeping up her body from her toes. She put down her glass and hugged her arms around herself to keep warm. He eyes misting, she wondered what would have happened if she had confessed to Richard that she had had a baby girl, years before. Funny how she never pictured her grown up. She saw her still as she was in the hospital, little blonde head, wide blue eyes, a little searching mouth. They had bound her breasts, and taken her baby away, saying that it was better for her not to see her again. She had wanted to die.

Her little girl would have been already ten when Richard wanted to adopt. Too late! Too late to take her from her parents.

She thought she had come to terms with her life until Audrey had come to see her. She had been deliriously happy with her first son, her husband so devoted to them both. She had not let the nurse they had hired do anything for young Ricky at first. All her frustrated mother love surged into adoration of Ricky. And then: the threat that this too would end. That Richard would despise her if he ever knew, that her family life would end — a fear suddenly ever-present.

She rose and poured another scotch. "Sophisticated Lady" mocked her in the background. Why should she have been the only one to suffer all these years?

She remembered how she had thrust Ricky abruptly at the nanny, and taken Audrey into the little den. And then begun paying, each month's check another stab of pain, a picking off of the thin scab over her hidden wound, till somehow, years later, there was a thick, unsightly scar in her soul, layer upon layer built up in order to protect Richard. While she, she thought, was past feeling.

Bill Barnes had just excised the scar. The original wound lay vulnerable, gaping, the pain returned. And just when she had thought she was healed.

She thought she would go mad if she had to go through all that pain again. She had borne it previously for Richard's sake, but he was gone. Oh, how she missed Richard! Her life was ordered now. Outsiders described it as "serene." Little did they know. Why had Richard died while Jamie Dewar continued to march through this world, receiving honors, arrogant, deceitful, rotten to the core of his being, but seemingly without pain?

She thought that perhaps he too could profit from a little, just a little pain. She put down her empty glass, picked up the telephone and asked the operator for directory assistance for Marlburg, Ontario.

CHAPTER TWENTY-TWO

Penny's hours were much different now that she was on Psychiatry. She had left the hospital at four o'clock, her day's work finished, and wandered home to do a laundry and have supper with her flatmates before going over to Andrew's Aunt Grace's with him.

Now Andrew and Penny were having their after-supper coffee with Grace, sitting in the small book-lined study, Grace's desk tidied after her day's work. A small sheaf of papers in a manila folder on one side supported her reading glasses, and the antique silver inkwell, ornately scrolled, its hinged top open, held a variety of modern ballpoint pens. One lay on top of her current manuscript. She had been interrupted while writing. But Grace did not mind such interruptions. Scientific correspondence, like Everest, would always be there, but the pleasure of having the young come to see you — Ah! There was a treat to be appreciated!

Penny always enjoyed going to Grace's. Grace intrigued her and she took great pleasure in interrogating the professor about her early life. "What had it been like to be one of the few female undergraduates at a university? Had she been treated differently? How did her professors react to her appearance in their classroom? Had anyone dared make remarks?"

On other occasions she would approach it from Grace's viewpoint. "Had Grace felt unique? Did she feel shut off from the usual pursuits of her highschool friends? Did she feel included in campus affairs? What were the other girls like? Had they been fuddy-duddies? What had she done for excitement in her spare time?" The questions poured out like silver droplets of mercury, coalescing into shining pools that would catch more reflections from the past.

"You must have felt like Madame Curie!" she exclaimed, as Grace laughingly described her surprise when her defense of her PH D thesis was held in front of a large audience, concerned more with the phenomenon of the defender than the defense.

"No, I didn't really feel discriminated against," she said. She had always just gone blindly ahead, not realizing that there were barriers she should not cross, and so the barriers had become just mirages, that faded into the distance as one came upon them, to be faced later by someone else who came along them on the road.

"Mind you, I'm not so brainless as to not know that there are barriers there for some women! A lot of them are bound by their social and cultural upbringing, but I was brought up to try and achieve anything I dared. Also, not having a family, I didn't have those hostages to fortune that chain some women. So you see," she continued, "I really had no possible excuse not to go on."

"And how had she come to be the first Dean of Women?" was Penny's next question.

Andrew sat back, amused by the turn the conversation had taken. Penny's questions often took him into un-familiar territory, for he never regarded Aunt Grace as anything but his great-aunt, a woman whom outsiders seemed to treat with admiration and respect.

It was hard for Andrew to disassociate himself from his childhood memories of her. As a very small boy, he had been a wanderer, to his mother's despair. Escaping from his own back yard at almost any opportunity, he could often been found at Grace's back door, honing in on Sarah's chocolate-chip cookies. And if he was lucky, his Aunt

Grace would be home, and there would be a bonus. Sitting perched on the stool in her study, waiting for his mother to retrieve him, he would find, tucked surreptitiously into his grimy fist, a small piece of toffee, or a licorice pipe, or his favorite, blackballs.

As he grew older and was allowed out by himself, the candy had remained the same, but the thrill of receiving it had diminished. But now he recognized the intrinsic charm of the ritual they had all played out. Sarah's role was to watch disapprovingly. "Spoiling that boy's teeth, I tell you," she would grumble. Grace would look down at his freckled upturned face, and they would smile, co-conspirators against authority.

In his teenage years there had been a temporary hiatus in his visits, for family had been something to grow independent of, to know more than, and he certainly wasn't about to go out of his way to seek out those few relatives he was not forced to associate with.

Although he now recognized that beyond the beaming smile and quiet manner lay erudition that would dazzle him, it had never occurred to him to ask his aunt any questions of the time before he existed.

Penny listened, appalled, as Grace described how she had come to know Margaret McDuff.

"You mean Miss McDuff had to take in a poor girl who'd been kicked out by her landlady because she was pregnant? How absolutely medieval! What happened to the guy? Have you ever heard of anything more antediluvian?" She set her jaw determinedly and turned to Andrew, expecting support.

She failed to get it. "Nothing ever happens to the guy. You know that," said Andrew. "He probably found a whole new hobby."

Penny gave him a scornful look. "That's just not funny, Andy!" she said. "I can't believe people with any sense ever accepted those hypocritical attitudes!"

"The girl was much happier living with Margaret,

Penny," said Grace pacifically. "She stayed there for three years after, until she graduated. Of course she had to give up the baby. One did, in those days. Never told her parents. Margaret was her substitute mother. Took her to the hospital. Made some lovely baby clothes. Helped deal with the adoption agency. I believe that after she moved away she got married and had a family. Margaret keeps in touch with her. Why, that baby could have children of her own by now! Funny, I can still see that little blonde fuzzy head!"

There was a moment's silence, which Penny ended with the question: "What were the medical students like in those days, Dr. Grace? How many women were in Medicine when you were an undergraduate?"

"None, child," laughed Grace. "Women weren't admitted to medical school in Canada, except to their own women's college. There were very few women in medical school in North America until fairly recently. Certainly, Lockland only admitted females after the war."

"Typically benighted!" declared Penny. "Especially when so many people prefer a woman doctor! I had a lady stop me in the hall the other day and tell me how glad she was to be examined by a woman doctor. She'd had a mastectomy a few years ago and she feels men just can't understand how she feels. Her surgeon thinks she should just get on with her life and she's ashamed to tell him how much the operation upset her. I don't see how men ever dared keep women out of Medicine!"

"When you've been around as long as I've been, you'll appreciate that changes come with time," remarked Grace. "We all get to fight some battles. You'll have your share, I'm sure," she sighed. She often wondered how the women of today would manage both career and home without the help that servants in her day had provided. "Did you have a very busy day today, dear?" she queried, changing the tone of the conversation.

"Not really," replied Penny. "I moved to Psychiatry yesterday. What a change from Obstetrics!"

"In what way?" asked Andrew.

"Well, it's so so much less hectic on Psychiatry, you'd think it would be relaxed. But it isn't! It's tense! I guess that's because any drama there is unhappy drama. But I shouldn't comment. I haven't been on it long enough to really assess it. I don't know, it's just that" — Penny was trying hard to explain her feelings — "although it's less work physically, it wears you out so much more mentally! I'm almost dreading being on call all weekend!"

Penny looked appealingly at her audience of two to see if they understood what she was trying to say. Her dark hair fell forward around her face and she tucked it back behind her ear.

"You can do it, Penny!" said Andrew. "They'll take one look at you and think they're lucky to be there!"

Looking at Andrew objectively, Grace thought that those kind of remarks showed he really didn't understand yet what Penny was facing.

Penny meanwhile was thinking back to her morning on the acute-care psychiatric floor. She thought especially of the man she'd admitted who had tried to commit suicide. She pictured him as she had seen him earlier, sitting apathetically on the side of the bed in the room closest to the nursing station, wrists bandaged where he had tried to slash them. He had been unable to speak without crying. The orders were to keep a constant watch on him. He was booked for his electroshock in the morning. She doubted if he could remember who had admitted him.

"I believe they have all kinds of new drugs out now for people with psychiatric illnesses," said Grace. "Isn't that so, Penny?"

"I think so," replied Penny. "They still rely on electroshock for the severe cases, but they have so many new psychotherapeutic drugs on the market now, that they've been able to close some of the wards in the psychiatric hospitals. Chronic schizophrenics are more able to cope in the outside world, and certainly the bi-polar disorders, as they call manic depressives now, are well controlled with lithium, in most cases."

"I was interested in reading about lithium," admitted Grace. "I suppose being a chemist I'm attracted to the elements. I've always felt that some of the mental illnesses are really a biochemical disorder. It seems so sad that we can use some drugs to do such good, while humans are doing such harm to themselves with all these street drugs."

"How's your work on drug abuse going these days, Aunt Grace?" asked Andrew. He had talked to her before about her involvement with a government-sponsored commission on Drug Abuse in Adolescence.

"Honestly, I feel like there's a world I don't know out there sometimes!" exclaimed Grace. "I can understand the teenagers feeling they are immortal and wanting to experience excitement. But when I think of those people who are profiting from the human misery they are causing, I have great trouble accepting the kind of immorality and avarice that is out there."

"Think of it in Freudian terms," proclaimed Andrew facetiously. "They failed to get enough chocolate-chip cookies in childhood! Look how that's kept me out of harm's way!"

Penny glanced at him and smiled. "What makes me think you don't want to be serious, Andy?" she inquired. "Could it be too much shop talk again? I do get carried away sometimes. How boring for you! It's as bad as discussing your lab work! Thermodynamics to the rescue!" She wrinkled her nose at him in some shared joke.

Grace looked lovingly at the two young people sitting side by side on her sofa. Oh, how she enjoyed those two! Andrew had always been one of her favorite grand-nephews, perhaps because he reminded her of his father as a young man. A little red-headed imp, his loving smile and winning ways had always made her forgive his childhood transgressions.

She wondered if Andrew and Penny's romance would

survive their separate fields of work. But Penny was right. These days women in Medicine were more accepted. And certainly Andrew had been brought up, both by precept and theory, to accept women's role outside the home, though at a pretty subconscious level.

She had always accepted the fact that Andrew had never thought about her own role in a man's world. To him she was primarily Aunt Grace, timeless, a certainty in his private world, there to provide cookies and entertainment for him when she was not away. Her life was but a satellite in his own constellation.

However, experience had taught Grace that Andrew was no different from most young men his age. The young usually saw themselves as the only ones who had ever been young, had ever loved, had ever struggled. They thought history began with them. But Penny was different — she had unusual empathy for her age, and a lively curiosity about her fellow human beings.

Eternally romantic, Grace hoped that Penny and Andrew would marry. Perhaps it was a long way down the road, if Penny wanted to graduate first, and with Andrew planning on post-graduate work. Penny would provide the human interest that Andrew would need to keep him as lovable as he was today. No Jamie Dewar he! Of course, Daphne and Eric had provided a loving, stable background for their children to grow up in. So unlike old Mr. Dewar!

The young today are more resilient, Grace thought. Unlike her own generation, there was not the compulsion to balance precariously on the prescribed, narrow walkway of societal rules. They could walk on a broader highway, and although the traffic was heavier, the options were greater. But, she caught herself, she was being fanciful. Penny and Andrew would decide for themselves in their own good time. Meanwhile, she had the pleasure of their company.

"Time to take the old girl home," said Andrew finally, watching Penny's long lashes slide shut and jerk open again. "Penny needs her beauty sleep!"

Grace looked at Penny. Something the girl had said had activated a distant, warning bell, like suddenly coming upon a solitary bell buoy clanging mournfully to and fro in the winter waves. Its alarm had sounded far back in the recesses of her mind throughout the latter part of the conversation, but it clanged more insistently, as if she were nearing danger, as Penny got to her feet, kissed Grace fondly on her faded cheek and said goodbye. Andrew took her hand as they walked, close together, down the flagstone path. Glancing back to wave a last goodbye, they found the front door still open and a pensive Grace silhouetted in the light from the hall behind.

CHAPTER TWENTY-THREE

Dusk had become night, and the moon risen high into a black velvet sky, before the phone call was eventually made. She did not want him forearmed with the knowledge of who was calling him. She was unwilling to risk the possibility that he would not speak to her if he was fore-warned, though she expected conceit would make him take the call. She remembered that popular song of a few years before: "You're So Vain!" It could have been written about Jamie.

She dialed.

Four long insistent rings before an angry woman's voice answered.

"Dr. Dewar, please. It's urgent!" she said breathlessly.

She could hear her in the background. "Jamie! Jamie! It's for you! Some woman, and she says it's urgent. It better be, to get God-fearing, hard-working folk up at this hour of the night!"

Then the deep, familiar voice, saying slowly, "Yes, Dewar here."

The words stuck in her throat for an instant, and she waited till she could control the cadence of her speech before she spoke.

"Jamie! My old friend! I don't think you remember me. You certainly didn't seem to recognize me at the alumni dinner. I didn't realize I had changed so much! Don't you remember me from your first year at Lockland, your friend Alice Muldoon?"

"Uh, no, no, I don't!" stammered Jamie, momentarily flustered, trying to remember the women he had seen at the alumni dinner. "Are you a trustee's wife?" There had certainly been that very attractive trustee's wife at the dinner but she had seemed to be avoiding him. Was she hoping he'd make the first move? If it was her, was she secretly interested in him now? He had known married women before who loved to play romantic hide-and-seek.

Then the realization of who Alice Muldoon was suddenly struck him, like a blow between the eyes. Good God no! Alice Muldoon! That innocent, half-baked first-year student from his undergraduate years? The stunning woman at the dinner couldn't be naïve little Alice! That woman was sophisticated! Had Alice been one of the waitresses? He hadn't noticed the waitresses. What did she want of him after all these years?

"No, not a trustee's wife, Jamie! A trustee, actually. You do seem to believe in stereotypes!" Her voice hardened. "I didn't get a chance to talk to you because I was so busy talking to another old friend. You knew her from your New York days, I believe! Audrey Benedict."

"Oh yes," said Jamie, automatically. "Very sad about Audrey!"

"Very sad!" echoed Alison. "She was such an imaginative lady, don't you think? I first met her while she was still in New York. I think you must have mentioned me to her. We've kept in touch over the years, of course. I wrote to her every month without fail."

"That's nice", said Jamie, leaning his forehead against the wall, his mind awhirl. How close had she and Audrey been? Audrey didn't associate with losers like little, naïve Alice. Suddenly another wave of memory struck him. He saw himself sitting in a chair in his and Audrey's apartment, looking at the social columns for prototypes whom he would one day emulate. When he read "Backstrom Heir

Marries Canadian in Society Wedding," he had been amazed to find Alice Muldoon of New Rockport named as the bride. He must have told Audrey about it. It was rather a coup to have known, rather intimately, in fact, the bride of one of New York's first families — before the groom did. That would have impressed even Audrey.

But Alice's voice jerked him back to the present. "Yes, the police informed me she even told her husband she would be spending convocation morning with me."

"You saw her convocation morning?" Alison could sense his rising awareness as Jamie's voice edged up nervously. "What did you tell the police?"

"I didn't tell the police anything, Jamie. I preferred to speak to you."

"Oh!" His voice steadied. She was still in love with him. After all these years!

"Yes. Audrey left me a little legacy for you, Jamie." She waited. The silence hung taut between them.

"What legacy?" The words rolled ponderously back across the wire, weighted with suspicion.

"I'd rather tell you in person about it, Jamie. Gift-giving is much more fun face to face, I always think. Can you meet me tomorrow night, Jamie? Or do you think I'm too forward, being the one to ask you for" — she hesitated momentarily — "an assignation?" Her voice lilted temptingly now that the message had been successfully delivered. She had been right in predicting that his vanity would prevent him from hanging up halfway through the conversation.

"Not at all," replied Jamie mechanically. "Could I take you out for coffee? Perhaps we could have dinner?" He was trying to think of a place he could take her where they would not be noticed. He would have to say he'd heard of an outstanding restaurant in a nearby town that he was dying to try.

"Oh, you're too kind!" she laughed. "I wouldn't impose on you to that extent. No, I just want to deliver my little reward. I'm so romantic, Jamie. Do you remember where we used to meet to avoid Mrs. Helland? No? I'm disappointed! It lives in my mind, I assure you! Behind the library, next to the fountain. Could we meet there tomorrow night at nine o'clock?"

"Delighted!" responded Jamie. Nine o'clock — if he was a bit late, it would be dark, and they would not be seen. His mind raced ahead. He'd better wear dark clothing, too. "Wear navy blue, for old times' sake!" he begged. "It goes so well with your fair hair." He was almost sure that she had had fair hair.

"Worried about recognizing me?" she said provocatively. "I don't think you need to. There won't be that many middle-aged women around the fountain at that hour, Jamie."

"On the contrary, you are unforgettable, Alice!" Jamie ventured. "I'm so delighted to talk to you again. I admit I hadn't dared hope for the pleasure of seeing you again, here in Marlburg, but I knew there was something about you that attracted me at that dinner." He realized Alice must have been the woman he'd thought was a trustee's wife. "It's been a long, long time, Alice!"

"It certainly has, Jamie!" she replied. "Sometimes it seemed like forever. But I've changed, you know. I'm not the fool I once was. Fair warning. Don't underestimate me, Jamie. I'll see you tomorrow, at nine, beside the fountain. I'll have your little gift with me. Until then, goodbye."

She put down the receiver softly. She hoped he would have a long night — one of those nights where sleep did not come, and only dawn dispersed the specters of despair circling the bed. She intended to sleep peacefully, his discomfort her soporific.

Still clutching the receiver, Jamie Dewar sank slowly into the chair beside the wall phone, staring blankly at the stained brown wallpaper. So Audrey had done it after all, taped their conversation in the maze. That was his legacy from Audrey — the missing tape, delivered by one of his previous lovers. Audrey's manipulations had always been skewed.

He had forgotten Alice. She had been so boringly naïve, so trusting. Inevitable that it had worn thin after a while. He had been glad to get away from both her and that tiresome biology assistant that summer. Whining and importuning him when he had so much on his mind! Just because she had shown him the exam questions.

Hard to know which of the two women had been more upset! Fortunately, that whole business with Alice had been settled by the time he'd come back to start second year. She must have miscarried. It would have been too hard for her to get an abortion in those Calvinistic days. He had only had glimpses of her after he came back. Scuttling around the campus, nervy and white-faced, she had avoided him. Just as well. He had been going places and she would have been a hindrance.

Amazing that she should have done so well. It showed what marrying into a rich old family could do. He imagined that it had probably taken them some time to bring her up to snuff. She was quite a looker now. He had always been able to pick them!

Except for Audrey. He should have expected this from Audrey. That bitch! He'd condemned himself in that recording. He wasn't going to be able to leave town. He had to get that tape back. Tomorrow! Before Alice Muldoon . . . Dear God, he wasn't sure he had her present name right, and he didn't know where she lived. What was her married name? It began with B, he was almost sure. Backstrom, that was it. Or was it? He tried to remember. He couldn't be sure. So how could he find her? Silence her? He would have to meet her as she had planned.

CHAPTER TWENTY-FOUR

The insistent brrr, brrr of the dial tone finally forced Jamie Dewar to hang up the dangling receiver. He walked back along the corridor to his room, ignoring his aunt who, clutching her housecoat around her, peered out of her doorway.

"Go to sleep, Aunt Dora," he said shortly. "It's got nothing to do with you."

He could hear her sharp intake of breath, and then the indignant, emphatic closing of her door. People did not speak to their elders in that tone, the sound implied, but he had other things on his mind.

He shut the door of the guest room and sank dispiritedly into the stiff, Victorian armchair, with the faded tapestry seat that his mother had worked, in another world, another time. Would she have cared that he was in trouble? Or had she been a true Dewar, concerned only with what the outside world would think of him?

She had died of breast cancer when he was five, and he had few memories of her. The one he had, he had striven to forget, for it upset him still as it had upset him long ago: her soft, hopeless crying, and his father saying that she wasn't to upset her sisters-in-law. Perhaps that was when she had realized fully she had not much longer to live. Perhaps she had minded leaving her little boy with her sisters-in-law.

Had she loved him? He could barely remember her

before her illness possessed her. He thought she might have cuddled him once or twice, surreptitiously. Not often, though.

More probably, she'd been much more like the rest of the Dewars. She had deserted him, hadn't she? She'd probably felt that he would be in capable hands. Who knew now?

All Jamie Dewar knew was that he was alone — and in potential trouble of a magnitude unlike anything he had previously encountered in his entire life.

He switched off the overhead light. He needed to think, and he needed to think undisturbed, without Aunt Dora coming in and wondering why he was wasting electricity. Besides, there was moonlight, clear, pale, searching moonlight, throwing the old farm outbuildings into sharp relief against the night sky, burnishing the dusty yard around the chicken coop with a silvery patina, streaming in his window to outline the ornately carved headboard of the double bed that had been his parents'.

Audrey had double-crossed him! She had taped their conversation in the maze. He had never imagined she would be so methodically calculating. Usually she lashed out instinctively. Perhaps she had been put up to it by Alice. He recalled now how absorbed in conversation she'd been with the woman he'd thought was a trustee's wife. They must have planned it then. Alice, that foolish village girl, metamorphosed into that attractive . . . no, he must have been euphoric that night. She was too vindictive to be attractive. Elegant, sophisticated, carefully preserved, yes. But not truly attractive.

He tried to recall their conversation in the maze. He had kept his voice down, but today's modern recorders with their sophisticated gadgetry could easily have picked it up. He had not said much. Audrey, however, had. . . . His train of thought veered right. Audrey had deliberately led him into a sequencing account of that episode with the old professor at Columbia. He'd had to do it! The old queer had favorites, and he was a tough marker. You did what you had to do in this world.

He should have denied the whole episode at the outset. But he had been astounded at the wealth of detail in her recounting. While she was talking, his mind had jumped ahead to a mental image of that story's impact on the General. General Powell, sitting in Head Office, issuing commands as if he were still in the army. If he was capable of decreeing Sunday-morning prayer breakfasts that were actually attended by the vice-presidents, if he could change the martini lunches to send-in working lunches, if he had fired O'Neill for lurching in to the cocktail party after the directors' meeting with a hooker on his arm, what wouldn't he do to Jamie if he got wind of that story?

And get hold of the story he would. Jack Mitchell would see to that! Up and coming, was Jack Mitchell. Butter wouldn't melt in his mouth. Bringing his Protestant high-society mother to Sunday prayer breakfast! In her best Westmount English, a string of fat pearls outlining her goiter, she'd had a lovely time talking to General Powell about the fundamentalist movement and the Moral Majority. No, if the General got wind of this story, the best Jamie could hope for would be to keep his job. And only because no scandals were allowed to surface in the General's august company! That was why the higher-ups in Switzerland had parachuted him in. To turn the company image around. Jamie knew what would happen. No advances. Shifted laterally into oblivion. Ignored at all policy meetings, watching younger men leap-frog past him. The last to be told and the first to be superannuated.

And what if Audrey herself had recorded other information on that tape to confirm their discussion? That elongated bundle of well-dressed bones, her horse teeth showing, would have been capable of anything!

She must have tried to protect herself by giving the tape to Alice. It didn't work, but she had tried. That much was evident. He had seen them talking together at the dinner. Saturday morning Audrey had told him she was going to see a friend before convocation, but that she would be there in time to see him perform. Confirmation. It must indeed have been Alice! Funny, he had never thought that Audrey and Alice were the least bit alike. But who could understand women? Obviously, they had planned the whole thing together.

Which meant that Alice, too, knew what was on the tape. But, if he got the tape away from her, then all she had was hearsay evidence. The General would never pay attention to that. There was always in-fighting in the company, and he always demanded concrete evidence. He trusted no one's word.

What if she had made a copy? His voice was distinctive, unmistakable. He would have to meet her and force her to give up all the tapes. He had too much to lose to let a little adventure with an old fag be exposed.

Even without scandal, lately things had been a little more rocky at work than usual. He had hoped getting an LL D would keep him on top of the pile a little longer. Thelma was readying the press release for the firm's internal newsletter now. He hoped she had been able to convince the reporters for the national newspapers to publish it as well. Even a small item in *Maclean's* or perhaps *Time* would be very useful.

Now he had to concentrate on how to get the tapes back. The method he used would be very important. Obviously he could get one copy of the tape back, but at what price? What would Alice demand? One episode of blackmail often led to further episodes, and one copy could lead to further copies. His solution would have to be definitive — final.

It would be stupid to underestimate the avarice of the woman just because her husband was rich. Perhaps her husband had tied up his money so she had no capital to spend.

If not money, he wondered what else she might want of him. He must find that out before he dealt with her. It is easier to deal with an enemy if you know him. Or her. Would she have a friend to whom she'd given a copy for safekeeping? He would have to be very gentle with her till he had mentally disarmed her.

If he were there by eight, it would still be light enough to get the lay of the land. Looking around in a library would not occasion any comment. So long as he wasn't seen with her. He should be able to look out a window at the meeting place. Had they really trysted at a fountain? How callow of him!

He had better not meet her until it was dark. It would make more sense, too, to wait until the library closed, and everybody had left, to ensure that they would not be seen together. Libraries, he suspected, closed at nine o'clock. He must check that out first.

So if he were there shortly after eight o'clock, he could reconnoiter. He could be watching for her arrival. He would stroll up to her, perhaps with roses, pink ones. Tell her how he had thought of her all these years. How he couldn't believe someone as attractive as she still was could be old enough to have been his contemporary. And that was why he hadn't recognized her. Although she was so irresistably attractive that he had been drawn to her as by a powerful, magnetic force.

He began to quite enjoy the scene. He would lead her to a bench. She would cry. They usually did. He would take his handkerchief out of his breast pocket and dry her eyes. Finally she would lay her head for comfort on his shoulder.

It might be quite a feather in his cap to resume relations with her. She was quite somebody now. She might be looking for another relationship. Her voice had sounded seductive until she had told him about Audrey's legacy. Then it had become threatening.

Prudence dictated that he deal with the immediate issue. He had to make plans, plans that would shut out the likelihood of his ever being blackmailed again. He shifted restlessly in his chair. He felt his age, for one of the first times in his life. It was getting harder and harder to remain on top of the heap.

He had always had contempt for those people who slid down from the summit, their fingers carving desperate grooves, their hands clawing to maintain their grip. But he had the sensation suddenly of his own hands loosening, scrabbling on the shale of the pile, could hear the pebbles dislodged by his effort rattling down beside him as he slid full length. For a brief moment, he could sense the desperation that would make someone give up and start the slide down . . . down . . . into oblivion. Plans. His head nodded.

He slept.

Barely dawn, and still slumped in the stiff old chair, Jamie jerked himself awake. Spine stiff and aching, he glanced down in amazement at his hands. His fists were clenched, his nails dug into his palms, palms made raw by the rapelling rope of the thought that he too might be beginning the long slide down from what he once was.

CHAPTER TWENTY-FIVE

The little librarian twittered nervously. Ten minutes to closing. She had cleared her throat officiously once already, hoping that the people still browsing would observe the sign that said: "Please have all books signed out ten minutes prior to closing." Still there were three or four persons making no effort to obey the sign. What a peculiar night it had been! A handsome, vaguely familiar man had wandered in, had stationed himself in true detective fashion, hands plunged deep in his trenchcoat pockets, back flattened against the wall, left profile turned, and had stared fixedly out the windows overlooking the back entrance, watching the sun set slowly behind the western hedges.

Whomever he was waiting for would be too late to take out any books; library rules demanded they close promptly at nine. The sun slid lower, the hedges darkened to the color of verdigris beneath the flaming sky. The little librarian became quite indignant. What right did he have to practice his spying here! He was not even making a pretense of looking along the shelves. This was a university library, not an espionage setting!

Suddenly, as if conscious of her eyes upon him, he turned and walked to the History section, fingering the spines of books in passing, as if he sought old friends. And then he was gone. She knew he had taken no books, although his trenchcoat looked bulky, as if he had concealed a parcel beneath it, but the bell, warning of a book theft, had not gone off.

The librarian suddenly flushed with embarrassment. It might have been a gun! What if the man was a real detective! They had had trouble with teenagers loitering in the courtyard recently. The janitor had even found beer bottles and other refuse around the fountain just last week. She had submitted a detailed report to the library board. Perhaps they had called in the police. A plainclothes detective! The thought gave her a delicious little thrill. How exciting!

Perhaps, though, he'd just been waiting for that other man who was absorbed in the Law section to leave. This was the second night he'd been looking through that particular section. On Tuesday he'd asked Ella about patent rights, and she'd shown him what they had. She had suggested that he go to the Law Faculty library, but he must have ignored her suggestion. Here he was again, thumbing through reference books, notes all over the table, his briefcase open untidily beside him.

The two men had not spoken to each other. In fact, it was more probable that they had not seen each other, what with one of them at the table in the reference section, muttering to himself, bent over his books, and the other staring continually out the windows at the back into the gathering gloom. He might be waiting for someone else entirely.

"I really think," she said determinedly to her young helper, "that you'll have to ask that man to make up his mind which books he wants to take out. Oh, and be sure to tell him he can only have two on any one subject."

The little blonde helper with the bee-stung lips twirled her bangle bracelets around on her arm, and started to move from behind the counter.

"Oh wait!" said the librarian. "Start with the two ladies. They're regulars, they won't mind. Mrs. Moses! Mrs. Moses! It's closing time!"

The little helper lowered her head and went back behind the counter to sign out Mrs. Moses' books. "I just love Ellis Peters' books," the girl gushed, putting the cards through the electronic card reader. "I think it's so nice to improve your mind when you're reading a murder mystery. It makes it seem so much more . . . decent somehow! Our English professor says they're quite accurate historically, and so cultured!"

"So is yoghurt!" said Mrs. Moses repressively. "I read for my own pleasure, young lady! I gave up worrying about English professors years ago. I suggest you do the same."

The man sitting at the long table in the Law section looked up in response and smiled. Good old Edwina Moses! One of Marlburg's grand dames, she didn't give a damn for anybody. Suddenly he caught sight of Jamie Dewar, raincoat collar up, leaving by the back stair. Jamie Dewar of all people, in the Lockland library, for Christ's sake! It was unlike the bastard to be doing his own research. So what was he up to?

Ray decided that it might be interesting to find out. He rose unhurriedly, gathering his papers and stuffing them into his briefcase, leaving the reference books strewn on the table. He went out the front door and walked nonchalantly down the front steps. Jamie, he knew, would eventually have to circumnavigate the building and exit from the back courtyard. He remembered the telephone booth half hidden in the cedars at the corner of the building. It would make a good observation site. Ray slid in and shut the door, keeping his head lowered as he pretended to be searching in the open directory.

The first surreptitious glance Ray took presented him with another surprise. A group of teenagers were congregated outside the courtyard wall. The girls were giggling at something one of the boys had said. One of the girls, wiggling with delight like a young puppy, was his own daughter. Vanessa must be out marching again, Ray thought, for Kathy to be out. Wasn't twelve a little young to be out with this gang? Those boys looked to be seventeen or eighteen.

But could he play indignant father at this stage in his life, he wondered. He had studiously avoided it so far.

He had experienced many new emotions in the last week. He had tapped a wellspring of unexpected enthusiasm for the game that he was now playing. Euphoria possessed him. It replaced the need to role-play the drunk, for now he could anticipate that shortly he would be revealed as a meritorious inventor who'd been badly cheated. And if it wasn't going to be possible at this late stage to publicly correct the wrong that had been done to him, at least he would be rich. He reveled in the mystification he was causing at home. He laughed out loud. He hadn't seen Vanessa so confused in years! She, who always had all the answers, before he even articulated the questions, didn't now know which end was up.

It seemed ridiculous to give all that up in order to play *pater familias* to this last little fledgling, preening her feathers before the young bantams. Probably the other kids had done the same in their day. In a large family such as he had come from the oldest always looked after the younger ones. Where were her older sisters now when they were needed?

Kathy would probably be ashamed of him if he suddenly appeared. It would look as if he had followed her. Generally he tried to spare the kids his public image. He looked down again, pretending to search the pages for a non-existent name.

One kid pulled a packet of cigarettes out of his back pocket and, with a self-conscious laugh, offered a cigarette to Kathy. Ray reared back, offended. When she took it, Ray almost left the phone booth. However, his preoccupation with Jamie Dewar's whereabouts stopped him. Jamie might appear from the back courtyard at any time. It was no time to be caught chastizing his daughter. The teenagers sauntered around the corner into the back and were lost to Ray's view. He waited.

The sky darkened dramatically, the moon obscured suddenly by a wisp of black cloud. Ray heard footsteps running past him, and then a scream, followed by more screams, tore the silence into which the teenagers had disappeared. A shadowy figure in a trench coat hurtled past the booth, and instinctively Ray dashed after it, his feet pounding frantically on the pavement.

The Faculty Wives' Association executive had ended a rather acrimonious meeting in the basement of the Lockland library. It was the final meeting before the summer hiatus, and in most members' eyes, it was one too many. They were looking forward to a peaceful summer, and the contemplation of fall commitments was distasteful. Most of the executive members had already climbed into their cars and pulled hurriedly out of the parking lot by the time Anne Levy, their president, and Helen Clay, their executive secretary, finally closed the books on the projected fall agenda.

The library lights were off, and the stairs lit only by the dim glow of a night light when they picked their way cautiously up the back stairs. Helen pushed the bar on the back door to emerge into the summer twilight, continuing to expound on the merits of her latest, summarily rejected plan. "I still think we should try a fashion show to raise money this fall," she expostulated, suddenly coming to a halt as she heard intermittent shrill screams interspersed among steady sobbing, much like flashes of lightning periodically subdivide the constant rumble of far-off thunder.

"Honestly, these teenagers! No wonder the librarian has been complaining to the janitor again. They should make the courtyard off limits to them," said Anne Levy astringently to Helen as they approached the group, some of whom were unaccountably kneeling by a dark blotch near the fountain.

Helen Clay hurried towards them in the semi-darkness, wobbling slightly on her high heels on the uneven flag-stones. It looked as if there might be trouble there, and what if her son Paul were among them? Directly opposite the group kneeling around the blotch, her heel caught in a crack between the stones and her ankle twisted. She fell to her knees.

Unexpectedly she found herself face to face with a woman, lying sprawled beside the fountain. Her navy blue raincoat flung dramatically open, the woman lay uncon-scious, spread-eagled on the cruel stones, her silk dress hiked above her knees. Her hair was matted with half-clotted blood, and her eyes rolled upwards, white under half-closed lids. Her face was ghostly under the night sky. Pink roses lay scattered like a pall about her. The teenagers bunched together for comfort.

Helen staggered to her feet and caught at her friend for support.

"Not again!" she murmured pitifully. "I can't go through it again!"

Anne gave Helen her patented, no-nonsense look, used so successfully on recalcitrant association members, and thrusting the books she was carrying at Helen, dropped to her knees beside the unconscious woman. The littlest teenager continued to sob, while a plump little blonde in a tight T-shirt held her mouth agape, screeching a methodical accompaniment.

"My God!" Anne Levy ejaculated in horror. With a tremendous effort of will, she regained her composure and assessed the situation. "You there," she said, pointing to the tallest boy, whose face was greenish-white, but who appeared most under control, "hammer on the library doors till someone lets you in. Then call an ambulance. Stop that howling," she demanded imperiously of the screeching girl. "And some of you go get me some water, Right there — from the fountain! And give me your handkerchiefs. . . . No, you wouldn't have any. Get me some paper toweling! She's still alive. I can feel a pulse. Helen, for God's sake, help me stop this bleeding!"

Helen had dropped the books nervelessly from her hands as the world spun and tilted around her. She tottered her way over to the side of the fountain, her knees unwilling to support her. Her groping hand touched something warm and sticky on the rim of the stonework. She looked at her upturned hand, red with clotted blood and hair in the moonlight, and slid quietly to the flagstones in a faint.

"Leave her!" commanded Anne Levy. "She's better that way! Help me to keep this woman warm! Don't move her till the ambulance comes!"

One boy took off his jacket and, gulping, wordlessly handed the jacket to Anne. Then he stepped back into the group.

The group of teenagers had split into two, those who huddled, fear-stricken, against the brick wall of the library, staring at the tableau in front of them, and those who were obeying Anne Levy's frantic commands. They could hear the far off wail of the siren coming closer and closer, and then the sound of rescuers approaching on foot.

"Thank God!" said Anne Levy to the ambulance attendants, as she slumped back on her heels and eyed the carnage. "I think this lady must have fallen against the fountain. She has a head injury. That one," she indicated Helen, lying in a crumpled heap, moaning quietly, "just fainted when she saw what had happened."

Working in the dimly lit courtyard, the ambulance attendants tended to the victims as best they could in the eerie green light that rose skyward from spotlights trained on the fountain from below. It lent an unearthly phosphorescence to the silhouettes of the men going about their work. The teenagers remained riveted to the spot. A police siren could be heard wailing nearby.

"What's going on here?" demanded a policeman, coming around the corner, gun drawn.

"Christ, who knows? This dame fell and hit her head on the fountain," replied an ambulance attendant, covering the woman on the stretcher with a blanket. "And that one fainted when she saw her. I don't know what the kids are doing here. . . . I wish to God that kid would stop that screaming! It's a madhouse around here!"

"Yeah?" said the policeman. "You should see it out front! We just arrested two men wrestling on the ground just in front of the library. No sooner do we separate them and haul them up, then one of them decks the other one. He goes down again, like he was pole-axed. When we help him up again, we see that the front of his raincoat is covered with blood. He's not bleeding and neither is the guy who hit him. He's going to have some explaining to do! Especially with her like that!" He jerked his thumb towards the stretcher.

The two oldest boys' eyes grew wide with excitement. This was the real thing!

Helen had come to and could be heard mumbling to herself. "It has to be an accident! It has to be an accident! It can't be murder. It mustn't be murder!"

Kneeling down beside her, Anne Levy put her arm around Helen's shoulders. "We'll take you to emergency, Helen," she said gently, "and get you a sedative. Don't worry! You'll be all right."

As she guided Helen out of the courtyard and around to the front where a second ambulance waited, the one containing Alison screamed off into the night. "Really!" Anne thought to herself, "You can't even have a quiet meeting around here anymore without something going wrong!" If there was going to be this much aggravation, she concluded, she might as well give up volunteer work and get something that paid.

CHAPTER TWENTY-SIX

Ted Clay walked numbly into his house in the early dawn, after taking Helen back to the hospital for the second time in one night. The sedation she had received on the first occasion in Emergency had had a paradoxical effect on her. The doctors' explanation was, that instead of sedating her, the drug had acted to release the tight control Helen was keeping on her emotions. He thought a simpler explanation was that she had become unhinged. He had not known how to cope with her frenzied, uncoordinated activity, and her recycling of the death scenes she had witnessed.

The second time she returned they had watched her in Emergency for almost an hour, reluctant to admit her, but she had gotten worse instead of better. They had thought the drug would wear off in time. Finally they had had to admit her to the Psychiatric floor, but only when she started to shy away from imaginary bodies she saw lying on their stretchers.

Ted felt he was living in a nightmare. It had begun the night before with Anne Levy calling him around eleven o'clock to tell him not to worry, but that Helen had fainted at her meeting. Anne was phoning from Emergency, where they had checked Helen over and given her some Valium. She thought Helen would prefer it if he came down and collected her, rather than have Anne drive her home. She was leaving now — could Ted be sure to come and get Helen?

He had left the two little girls, still up, amiably squabbling over the Monopoly board, and had driven down to Emergency. Poor Helen! First there had been Audrey Benedict's untimely demise in the seat next to her. Now this!

The executive meeting had been Helen's first public appearance since convocation. She, who had always been a decisive person, had taken an incredibly long time deciding what to wear. Ted was usually oblivious of her wardrobe, but by the time she had finally put on her new linen suit and her beige and white two-tone shoes, he had felt like cheering.

"You look very elegant, Helen," he had said, placatingly. "You look pretty, Mummy!" Pammy, the more vocal one, had dutifully added. Nancy, the quiet one, more like her dad, had looked up briefly and smiled sweetly at Helen. "When are you coming home, Mummy?" she had asked.

"Mrs. Levy is picking me up to take me to the meeting, dear," she had replied, "and she'll bring me home as soon as the meeting is over. You be good girls for Daddy!" She bent to kiss them. They had heard Anne honking her car horn outside.

"We really have to start thinking of our fall commitments tonight," she had said to Ted. "But the meeting's sure to end before nine, because we have to be out of the library by then. Anne is driving. I don't want to take the car out. I still feel too nervous to drive."

Ted had looked a mite rebellious at the responsibility she was saddling him with. She had hastened to reassure him. "I'll be right home after the meeting, unless, of course, Anne wants to discuss some things privately with me. The children can put themselves to bed. They don't need a bath tonight. Paul will be home soon, probably. Tell him he can heat up his supper in the microwave. He must be studying late again."

When Ted had driven down to the hospital after Anne's call, Paul had not been heard from. Ted had been startled by the change in Helen's appearance since she had said goodbye after supper. Her suit was dirty and crumpled. Her psyche seemed to have crumbled too. She had gone to the car, walking like a somnambulist, holding one hand out in front of her, palm up, as if it were not part of her body.

But worse was to come. She had ignored the children's "Hi, Mummy" and had gone straight to the bedroom, where she stripped off her linen suit, bundled it into a plastic bag and shoved it into the darkest recess of the cupboard. Then she had put on winter underwear, her corduroy slacks and a thick, hand-knitted Norwegian sweater. She completed her ensemble with a solitary woolen glove.

"Why are you wearing winter clothing?" he had ventured to ask.

"It's freezing in here," Helen replied, going over to the thermostat on the wall and turning the furnace on.

"It's almost June!" he had protested, but she only said, "I don't care. I'm cold! So cold! I feel like a dead body!" She shivered.

He had not dared ask about the single glove on her right hand. He watched her for the next hour, pacing up and down, turning on the kettle for a cup of tea that she forgot to pour, crossing her arms and rubbing her shoulders as if it were indeed midwinter and she were chilled to the bone.

"This time you could see the blood," she muttered to herself. "It was all over her hair and the ground and even on the edge of the fountain. . . ."

Finally he had called their family doctor, who, remembering Helen's last attack of hysteria, had advised Ted to return her to the hospital.

Now it was four in the morning, and Ted was too exhausted to sleep. His daughters had put themselves to bed. Pammy, in her nightie, was peacefully asleep. But Nancy still had tear stains on her cheeks, and her faithful old teddy bear clutched feverishly to her chest. He did not bother to undress Nancy and put her into her nightgown. Instead he pulled up the blankets and turned off the light, remembering to switch on the nightlight. Nancy was prone to nightmares.

Ted wandered into Paul's room, and stopped, horrified, inside the door. Helen must indeed have been distracted this past week for her to let Paul get away with leaving his room in a state like this! Normally, and Ted could hardly remember when their life last had been normal, she insisted that Paul's room be reasonably clean and that he make his bed. Lately, she had conceded in part, and had been making his bed for him. She said he was so busy studying that she did not want to impose more duties on him. Ted wondered about that. If Paul was studying so blasted hard, why were his grades falling off?

Paul certainly was hard to wake up in the mornings now. Sullen, uncooperative, slamming out of the room if he was asked a question, rotten to Pammy and Nancy. . . . Helen said he was being a typical teenager. Ted had been an only child. He could never remember having been like that.

Mechanically Ted began to hang up the jeans lying on the floor. He threw the dirty underwear into the hamper, the crumpled-up notes into the wastepaper basket. He pulled up the blankets and found girlie magazines sticking out from under the mattress. There were deodorant sticks, a half-eaten apple, matches, a stained kitchen knife, a roll of paper toweling, and a safety razor among the debris on the desk. Gathering up all the bathroom paraphernalia first, Ted carried a huge armful into the bathroom.

Past 4:00 A.M. and Paul was still not home. Ted was responsible for a son who was only sixteen, and he did not even know where to begin looking for him. Helen was the one who normally did that.

Ted became acutely aware of every car driving by on the street outside. As each car approached, it would seem to Ted, ears straining, that it was slowing directly in front of the house. He'd tense, anticipating the thud of the car door closing, and Paul's key turning in the lock. But, as he began rehearsing his speech to Paul, he would hear the car continue on its way, the sound diminishing in the distance.

He wondered if Helen had the gift of looking into the future. Was it Paul's body that she had seen lying on the emergency-room stretcher? Was that why she cracked? What if he did not know where Paul was by morning? What if Paul did not call? What if he had to tell Helen that Paul was dead? Ted thought that the night's stresses were driving him crazy too. He forced himself to keep busy until Paul came home. He could not bear to lie alone in bed and think.

At 5:30 A.M. Ted was cleaning the bathroom vanity in order to put away Paul's belongings. "Wait till I get that kid home," he repeated to himself, tossing old razor blades and empty shampoo bottles into the wastepaper basket. "Wait till I tell him what he's done to his mother. . . ." There was a pleading, prayerful component to his parental incantation, much like that of people who bargain, "Please God, if you let Johnny live, I will do such-and-such."

The wastepaper basket grew more full, the vanity more empty. The shelves were finally clear. Ted looked behind the U-pipe draining the basin for the cleaning cloth that Helen kept tucked there. Pulling the cloth out he felt something wrapped in it. He looked. It was a syringe.

Ted sat down abruptly on the bath mat. He now had an explanation for Paul's peculiar behavior. Paul was shooting drugs.

CHAPTER TWENTY-SEVEN

Sarah had gone to the early service at church as usual. Grace was happily puttering in her perennial bed, identifying emerging delphiniums and lupins, when she heard the distant peal of her front-door bell above the chatter of the cardinals and jays at the feeder.

"What now?" she asked herself, hurrying in the back door, muddy trowel still in hand. She opened the front door to find Ted Clay on her doorstep. For an amazed moment she thought to herself that here was a perfect example of Providence at work, for Ted was one of Marlburg's foremost gardeners, and she had just come across a pale green, curling leaf she suspected was a fern but did not recognize.

Translating her thoughts into words, she exclaimed welcomingly, "Ted Clay! An answer to a prayer. There's a plant in my perennial border that I'm almost sure is a fern, but it might be a weed, and I'm not sure enough which it is to deal with it. Have you a moment to identify it for me?"

Mechanically Ted agreed, but it was obvious that he was distracted. Grace bustled him out to her back garden, chit-chatting about the the need for rain, and did he think one could plant annuals this weekend, and how the nurseries weren't selling their flats of impatiens yet. Did he think it was too early? Normally, she knew, Ted was uncomfortable unless talking about plants, so she chattered gaily on, as she wondered what it was he really wanted. Ted answered her abstractedly.

"You should ask them to hold the impatiens till next week, Dr. Grace," he said. "Just tell them now what colors you want."

He arrived at the edge of her perennial border, so obviously ill at ease and worried that Grace felt like a nineteenth-century mistress of the manor, about to chide the gardener's assistant for not dead-heading the roses properly.

"There's something bothering you, isn't there, Ted?" she asked gently. "Can you tell me what's wrong?" Fern or weed forgotten, she led him to where there were some garden chairs under the lilacs and sat him down, placing herself opposite him, her brown eyes full of concern.

"I hope so!" replied Ted. She could almost visualize him twisting his cap in his hands and saying. "Sorry, Ma'am. I didn't mean to offend." She wished she did not have this ability to paint unsummoned scenerios with that part of her brain not actively involved in dealing with the crisis at hand. It was an involuntary mental game that her mind played, like the physical ones children play where they simultaneously pat their head and rub circles on their tummy. She repeated: "What's wrong, Ted?"

"All sorts of things are happening that I don't understand," said Ted, his voice quavering. Ted was unaccustomed to voicing his thoughts. His speech was like a rollercoaster, gathering speed down the steep inclines, then hesitating at the bottom before gathering momentum to slowly chug up to the top again. It stilled for a moment before the final hurdle, then gathered enough momentum for him to unburden himself. He spoke in a rush.

"Poor Helen is in hospital with a bad case of nerves. I took her in last night. She and Mrs. Levy were coming out of the library after a meeting, and they stumbled across a woman who had been assaulted. Helen doesn't even know the woman, but I guess it brought back the memory of seeing Mrs. Benedict's body. Helen was very disturbed by that. Anyway, she fainted. So Mrs. Levy took Helen to the hospital to get a sedative. But she reacted to the sedative, and although I brought her home, I had to take her back, and they finally admitted her."

He stopped for breath.

Grace leaned forward towards Ted and said, "I'm so sorry, Ted! Do you need any help with the children or the house? I'm really not very experienced with children, but I'm sure Margaret would be glad to come back, and I'll certainly help her."

Ted seemed surprised by the suggestion. "No, no, we're managing fine," he said hurriedly. He went on to explain. "Helen always has a few casseroles in the freezer and we can put them in the microwave. And I'm not teaching at present."

"Well, do you want me to go visit Helen?" asked Grace, puzzled. As she was not particularly acquainted with the Clay family, she was beginning to run out of speculations about what Ted needed from her.

"It's Paul!" Ted blurted out, his voice quavering again. "My son," he explained to Grace's look of inquiry. "He's on drugs, and I saw in the paper that you are working on a drug commission."

"He's on drugs?" repeated Grace. "What kind of drugs?" She peered at him shortsightedly, realizing that she had forgotten to put on her glasses. No wonder she had had trouble recognizing that plant.

"I don't know," confessed Ted desperately. "He could be on anything, and with Helen in the hospital, I have all this responsibility!"

"What makes you think he's on drugs?" asked Grace, putting her gnarled hand on Ted's knee. The pervasive smell of the lilacs hung in the air, and a robin hopped inquisitively up to them, its head cocked to one side. The conversation seemed incongruous in that setting.

"He didn't come home last night!" admitted Ted.

Grace sat back in her chair and took a deep breath. "That doesn't necessarily mean he's on drugs," she explained. "He probably phoned to tell you where he was staying while you were still at the hospital. Or did you ask Helen? She might have given him permission to stay at a friend's." Poor Ted, she thought to herself, he certainly was not coping at all well, despite his protestations.

"You don't understand!" said Ted desperately. "I was waiting for him to come home last night, and I was tidying up." He gulped and stopped.

"Yes?" Grace prompted gently. It was obvious Ted would have to tell the story his own way.

"I was cleaning up his room. I took some of his things to put in the children's bathroom. I was worried about him and I couldn't sleep, so I cleaned out under the vanity." He stopped again. "It's not marijuana," he said. "It's heroin!"

"Heroin?" repeated Grace. Dear Lord, a quiet Sunday morning in her own garden, and she was hearing tales of heroin use in quiet old Marlburg. "What could possibly make you think that?"

Ted was silent again, marshalling his thoughts.

"Has Paul ever come home acting peculiarly?" she demanded. "Are there needle tracks in his arms? Come on, Ted! What makes you suspect your son" — "how old is Paul?" she interjected — "is involved with heroin?"

Ted looked at her with tears in his eyes. "It's so awful!" he said. "He's sixteen and he's been acting peculiarly for weeks!" The roller-coaster braked to a halt and then started up again. "He stays out late, he's rude to his mother, his room is a mess!"

"Well, that sounds pretty normal for a teenager, I'm afraid," said Grace. "That doesn't make him a heroin user!"

"Dr. Grace!" explained Ted at last, with conviction. "I cleaned up the vanity last night while I was waiting for Paul to come home and I found he had hidden a syringe behind one of the pipes! A used syringe!"

"Oh!" said Grace, momentarily silenced.

"I've come to you," he said, "because I don't want to tell the police about Paul. He's so young. He needs help, and I thought you would know where I could go to get it. His mother mustn't find out. He's her favorite. It would kill her!"

"Oh, poor Ted!" said Grace with ready sympathy. "Are you sure the syringe belongs to Paul?"

"Yes," he said quietly, "Nancy and Pammy are too young." His face was drawn with despair.

Grace thought for a moment. "Leave it with me," she said finally. "Don't say anything to Paul. I'll try to find out exactly what's the best thing to do."

Ted rose from his chair. "Thank you" he said. "I'd better be getting back. The girls haven't had breakfast yet."

Grace sat for a long time in her study after Ted had gone. "Always presume innocence until guilt is proven." Her scientific training reasserted itself. There might be other explanations. But what other explanations could there be?

Sarah appeared at the study door. "I'm home!" she announced unnecessarily. "You should have seen the hat Mabel Percival was wearing today! She had everything on it but the kitchen sink! And I might just have missed that!" She smiled happily to herself at the memory.

"Oh!" she added importantly. "Somebody had flowers on the altar in memory of that Mrs. Benedict! It can't have been her husband. He don't even go to our church!"

Grace stood up decisively. "I have to go out for a while, Sarah," she said. "I'll just get changed and go."

"I didn't know you was planning on going out!" said Sarah suspiciously. She didn't like the look on Grace's face. "Lunch is in an hour!" she warned.

"I'll be longer than an hour, Sarah," replied Grace. "I'm sorry. Go ahead without me. I don't know how long I'll be."

The taxi had taken Grace to the front entrance of the hospital. Information had supplied the floor and room number of the person she wanted to talk to. Grimly, she walked down the long, blank, windowless corridor leading to the elevators, her mind in turmoil. The light above the elevator lit up "1" and the elevator doors opened to disgorge a group of laughing student nurses. Grace slid in and flattened herself against a stretcher. An orderly was chatting to the accompanying nurse, as if the man lying there, blood running through tubing into his arm, was not present. "I danced for three sets," he said, with a smile. "My feet were killing me!"

The elevator stopped. Grace watched the indicator light. Eight. Not her floor. Still chattering, they trundled the man on his stretcher away. The doors slid shut. She shot upwards.

The indicator arrow changed from the green "Up" to the red "Down" and the elevator stopped. Grace emerged alone onto the tenth floor. There was a beautiful view from the windows. She could see half of Marlburg and the Washigon River through the bars.

Grace found Helen alone in her room near the common room. Her door was open. She was sitting passively in a chair, staring vacantly out the window. Grace could hear her talking to herself. "I didn't think there would be so much blood. Blood washes away the sins of the world. If there had been blood the first time. . . ."

Grace interrupted her. "Hello, Helen," she said. "I'm Grace Forrester. I don't know if you remember me, but I gave a talk at a Faculty Wives' meeting last year. You arranged it. You were the program organizer, I believe."

Helen looked at her without changing expression. Her eyelids were heavy, hooding her glazed eyes. No spark of recognition flickered behind her glance. Grace thought she must be well sedated. "Oh yes," Helen replied listlessly. "I remember. You talked to us about teenagers and drugs."

"Yes, I did," agreed Grace. "And I've come to talk to you again today."

"You don't have to. My children don't take drugs!" It was a flat denial.

"Actually, I'm not going to talk to you about your children or street drugs," said Grace. "I thought I should talk to you about the medical drug that I think killed Audrey Benedict. I think you might know something about its use." She stopped and watched Helen get out of her chair and start to shuffle towards the bed.

"I don't know anything about succinylcholine," said Helen hastily. "Or how it works. I can't help you at all. Can't you see I'm sick? I've suffered a terrible shock. I really can't talk to you."

"But I never mentioned the name of the drug!" said Grace. "Helen, how did you get hold of it? Did you pick it up when you were volunteering at the psychiatric hospital? Is that how you got it?"

Helen came back to where Grace was sitting. A cunning look crept over Helen's face. "What makes you think it would be me?" she asked. "Lots of people volunteer at the psychiatric hospital."

"But only a very few would know how it works and for what purpose it is used. It's used to paralyze the patients before they get electroshock, isn't it, Helen?" demanded Grace. "You'd know. You're a nurse by profession, aren't you?"

"You can't prove it was me!" said Helen. "I didn't kill Audrey Benedict. You're just trying to upset me, because I'm in hospital and sick. You don't like me. I'm not important enough for you. You just want to find someone to blame. But I'll show you. I'm going to be very important some day, and I'm not going to be anybody's scapegoat."

"Helen," commanded Grace sternly, getting up from her chair and putting her face closer to Helen's. She leaned forward towards her for emphasis, trying to force some glimmer of understanding from her. "Listen to me! Your husband found a used syringe hidden in your bathroom. They're going to want you to explain that. If the police laboratory finds Audrey Benedict's blood on that needle, I'm afraid. . . ."

But she got no further. There was a sudden, defiant, warning flare behind the blue eyes, before Helen forced her backwards onto the bed, her hands gripping Grace's throat. There was an audible crack as Grace's wrist bent back under her. Grace felt intense pressure behind her eyeballs, the vise around her throat tightened, and as the blackness descended, her other hand groped for the bellcord and found it.

CHAPTER TWENTY-EIGHT

Grace sat primly across from Bill Barnes and David Merritt a few days later, a sling holding her casted arm across her chest. Fingers of her good hand pressed firmly against her lips, she was listening absorbedly as Dave Merritt spoke.

"I'm so impressed, Dr. Forrester," he was saying. "I'm still not sure how you made the connection between Mrs. Clay's volunteer job and the use of succinylcholine chloride."

Grace shifted her right hand to her elbow to lend support to the sling. Her cast felt heavy, her wrist still quite painful. Another six weeks, Dr. Day had said. He had also said, "Grace, is it impossible for you to stay out of trouble? Just give me a little warning the next time you try to solve a murder all by yourself, and I'll lay in a fresh supply of plaster of paris."

She had tried to defend her motives, explaining that she felt so sorry for Mrs. Clay, that she had wanted to make sure she was not accusing an innocent person. Dr. Day had been more understanding than Sarah. Sarah had acted as if Grace had deliberately misled her. It had taken her hours to explain why she hadn't taken Sarah with her for protection. She doubted if she'd convinced Sarah yet, for Sarah had taken to hovering again, as if she felt she couldn't trust Grace out of her sight.

It was Sarah's suspicious nature that had led to the detectives being ensconced in Grace's study, when she could just as easily have taken a taxi down to the Marlburg Police Station. She would have had to bring Sarah along on the journey, however, and that would have been a bit much, she thought.

"Well," she explained, "I probably wouldn't have made the connection if Dr. Clay hadn't come over to the house and told me about finding the syringe. He thought his oldest child was on drugs, and since I'm on a drug commission, he came to find out what he should be doing to help his son. After he left, I got to thinking about the other possible explanations for that syringe being hidden in the children's bathroom. Dr. Clay had told me his wife was distraught and in hospital — I began wondering if she were very ill, if she would be helped by electroshock, and then, suddenly, *voila!*" Grace waved her good hand in the air, then waited a moment to collect her thoughts before explaining how she had arrived at her conclusion.

"I remembered they give electroshock at the psychiatric hospital as well, of course," she went on. "I know you were looking for the place it was taken from, hoping that knowing who had access to the drug would help you identify the murderer, and I can't believe I didn't make the connection earlier! Anyway, I suddenly remembered about the psychiatric hospital, and then, I suppose because it was all in conjunction with Helen Clay anyway, I remembered she had worked there and I realized she probably had access to the drug."

She stopped and waited for their comments.

"Maybe it would have been better if you had just mentioned that to me, Dr. Grace," said Bill, looking reproachfully at her cast.

"Not you too, Bill!" exclaimed Grace in exasperation. "I've had Sarah down my neck ever since it happened. You see," she went on in justification, "I wasn't sure when I went to the hospital that it was Mrs. Clay. I realized she had the opportunity to get the drug, and probably to administer it, but I couldn't think of any reason she would have to kill Audrey Benedict. I didn't want to accuse an innocent woman, especially one that had had a nervous breakdown. And I still don't know why she did it!"

She turned to Bill for an explanation.

"It doesn't make much sense, Dr. Grace," he said. "I've talked to her a few times, and she keeps insisting it was justified. Helen Clay says that Mrs. Benedict was deliberately and systematically destroying her family. That's her motive. She told me that Mrs. Benedict had coerced her husband into not promoting Dr. Clay, that she had influenced the members of the Faculty Wives' Association to vote for Mrs. Levy instead of her for president, and finally that Mrs. Benedict was selling drugs to her son, Paul."

He did not mention that Helen Clay seemed to have transferred her animosity to Dr. Forrester, declaring that Dr. Forrester was also in the drug trade, supplying the high-school students with drugs when she went to give talks on drug abuse in the schools. He thought that item of news would be better suppressed. He looked at Dr. Forrester's left wrist, encased again in plaster, and thought that perhaps she might have gotten the message that Helen Clay did not care for her, anyway.

"She'll never be allowed to stand trial, Dr. Forrester," interjected Merritt, busily tamping tobacco into his pipe. "The doctors tell us she is a paranoid schizophrenic, who's decompensated and slipped over the edge. She'll be committed to a mental institution. She's not fit to stand trial."

"That's probably the kindest solution," remarked Grace philosophically, "although I do worry about how Ted Clay will cope. I wonder what sent her over the edge?" she asked.

"I can answer that," said Bill. "It was sitting next to Mrs. Benedict. She had it all planned to inject her with the drug at the reception after graduation. Then. . . ."

"How did she know she'd bother going to convocation?" interrupted Dave.

"I don't think Helen could imagine anyone not wanting to go to convocation. It is one of the social events of the university calendar," said Grace, pityingly.

"Anyway," continued Bill, "she came into the lobby after checking on the reception arrangements and saw Audrey Benedict waiting in the lobby. It was crowded, and she had the syringe already loaded, so all she had to do was to take it out of her purse. She managed to get right behind her, and jabbed the needle into her arm from close range. She says Mrs. Benedict flinched a bit, but didn't even turn around. Mrs. Clay could see the procession coming down the corridor, and she hurried in with the other people to her place before the procession came in."

"So why did she fall apart afterwards?" asked Dave. "It didn't seem to bother her while she was doing it."

"She wasn't expecting to have Mrs. Benedict come and sit down next to her," explained Bill. "That wasn't part of the plan. She had to sit there and pretend there was nothing wrong, while all the time she knew that Audrey Benedict was slowly suffocating to death."

"And then she had to get up and act surprised, I suppose," commented Dave, sucking on his pipe, with what he fondly imagined was his Sherlock Holmes look.

"Oh, dear!" said Grace, unhappily. The two detectives gave her a curious glance, for she had seemed quite inured to tales of violence up to that point, and they had not tried to protect her sensibilities.

"Oh, don't mind me," she said, apologetically. "I was just reminded of something the chaplain said to Margaret McDuff the other day." She went on to explain. "The chaplain annoyed Margaret by saying that women may murder but they don't like to see the consequences of their actions. We pooh-poohed that, and now look! It's true!"

Bill found it necessary to defend womankind. "This is a special case, Dr. Grace," he started, but suddenly stopped. What was he going to say next? That most murderesses he had known had loved to watch? Dave smiled to see his perturbation and mercifully changed the subject.

"Strange that we have two crimes we're investigating that we're not going to get to trial, isn't it?" he commented. –

Grace looked at him inquiringly.

"The assaulted woman Mrs. Clay found, bleeding by the library fountain, is one of the university trustees," he explained.

"Yes, that's Alice, I mean Alison, Backstrom," said Grace. "Margaret told me she was in hospital. I didn't know she was assaulted! What happened?"

"We don't know — officially," said Bill, gravely. "She was found unconscious by the fountain, covered in blood, and there was blood and hair all over the rim of the fountain. She recovered consciousness the next day, but she swears she's amnesic about the entire affair. Can't even remember what she was doing there, she says."

"She probably doesn't want the notoriety," said Dave. "If she pressed charges, she'd have to testify in court. The man is famous. It would hit the front pages, and she'd be a marked woman all the rest of her days. She doesn't need that!"

"I can't help wondering why she would agree to meet Dr. Dewar, though," mused Bill. "She told me she hated him."

"She probably does," agreed Dave. "She's not going to tell you what she planned on doing when they met. But I have a feeling whatever it was it made him very angry."

"Why do you say it's a crime if you haven't any proof?" demanded Grace, her scientific mind still in play.

"Because we arrested two men on the front lawn of the library who were fighting, Ray Clark and Dr. Dewar. Dr. Dewar had Mrs. Backstrom's blood all over the front of his coat and his hands. We think they had an assignation — there were roses scattered all around her — and that he got angry and slammed her head against the fountain. Probably not premeditated. He must have lost his temper at something she said."

"He denies it, of course," Bill continued as Dave became

preoccupied with relighting his pipe. "Says, yes, they arranged to meet, that they were old friends, and that she lost her footing, and when she fell and he saw all the blood, he lost his nerve and ran away."

"Jamie never lost his nerve in his entire life," commented Grace, rather uncharacteristically severe.

"I know," Dave went on, drawing on his relit pipe, "but we can't prove it. You can't arrest a man for being a coward."

"Why in heaven's name were Ray Clark and Jamie Dewar fighting on the front lawn of the library?" asked Grace.

"Don't know that either," answered Dave. "Neither one of them will say. The officers who arrested them put them both in the jug in Denham overnight. Dr. Dewar was pretty desperate by morning, before his lawyer came and posted bail, but Ray Clark seemed pretty happy."

"You mean he was drunk?" asked Bill, who had not heard the whole story. The uniformed branch had been in charge of the investigation.

"No, sober as a judge, according to Pete Hawkins," replied Merritt. "He had a few little private conversations with Dr. Dewar during the ride to Denham, and in the drunk tank, where they put them first. Came out very happy, just like he went in."

The two detectives got up to leave, more of their questions answered than they had dared hope. As Grace walked them to the door, under Sarah's watchful glare, she imparted a little gossip that Sarah had told her earlier.

"I think Ray's come into some money," ventured Grace. "Sarah says that their youngest daughter, Kathy, has been telling everybody that her father has sold the rights for a new drug process to Dr. Dewar's company, and that they're all going to be rich."

"If that's true, I wonder why Vanessa Clark isn't happier," commented Bill. "My wife says Vanessa Clark's going around acting as if Ray had taken up doing abortions."

FREE!!
BOOKS BY MAIL
CATALOGUE

BOOKS BY MAIL will share with you our current bestselling books as well as hard to find specialty titles in areas that will match your interests. You will be updated on what's new in books at no cost to you. Just fill in the coupon below and discover the convenience of having books delivered to your home.

PLEASE ADD $1.00 TO COVER THE COST OF POSTAGE & HANDLING.

- -

BOOKS BY MAIL
320 Steelcase Road E.,
Markham, Ontario L3R 2M1

IN THE U.S. -
210 5th Ave., 7th Floor
New York, N.Y., 10010

Please send Books By Mail catalogue to:

Name _____
          (please print)
Address _____

City _____

Prov./State _____ P.C./Zip _____

(BBM1)